Tree Fever

Tree Fever

Karen Hood-Caddy

RENDEZVOUS
PRESS

Book design: Craig McConnell
Cover photo: H. Mel Malton
Cover art: Jeff Miller,
                  RR #4, Limberlost Rd.
                  Huntsville, ON P0A 1K0
Poem *Lost* from the collection *He Who Shall Be the Sun*
by David Wagoner

Published by RendezVous Press
an imprint of Napoleon Publishing
a division of Transmedia Enterprises Inc.
Toronto, Ontario, Canada

Printed in Canada

05 04 03 02 01   5 4 3 2

Canadian Cataloguing in Publication Data

Hood-Caddy, Karen, date
        Tree Fever

ISBN 0-929141-53-9

I. Title.

PS8565.06514T73   1997   C813'.54   C97-930136-X
PR9199.3.H66T73   1997

To Florence, Clendon and Gwen
for the imperative.

To Austin, Gloria, Irma, Jason, Jean, Judith, Judy, Lizzy,
Margaret, Mary, Randi, Renae, Susan and Tia
for their support.

Special thanks to Jack McClelland for believing,
Sylvia McConnell for risking and
Mel Malton for nearly everything else.

This book is dedicated to all trees everywhere.

If what a tree or bush knows
is lost on you
then you are lost.
Stand still.
The forest knows where you are.
You must let it find you.

– a native elder's advice to a
young boy lost in the woods

Chapter 1

I awoke to the sound of lake water lapping, the primal, sloshing rhythm of water as it meets the shore over and over again. Sitting up, I opened my eyes. Sprawled before me, the luminous, naked body of the lake shimmered and shook in the rough embrace of Muskoka rock.

Blue, orange, purple-black and green, the water rolled towards me. Only a few weeks ago, the lake was held prisoner under ice that cracked and snapped like a whip keeping an animal in submission. But now the water was free again and rambunctious, slapping and clapping restlessly against the dock. Sometimes in its rollicking, splashes of water leapt into the cool spring air, breaking into a spray of silver droplets that sparkled in the light.

Wrapping a blanket around me, I moved to the open window. The waving arms of a thousand evergreens greeted me. I breathed deeply as though I might draw the lush smell of them into the landscape of my body.

Should I go for a swim? If anything could pull the sluggishness from my body it would be the coldness of the lake. It would wake me up, get me going. I'd slept in again. Why was it so hard to get up lately? And when I was up, I couldn't get myself going. A swim would be perfect. Years ago, I started every day with a swim.

My shoulders hunched and my fingers pulled the

blanket more securely around me. My body did not like this idea. Is this what aging does, makes you decide things because of temperature? Comfort? Disgruntled, I sighed and stared out at the lake.

In the dark-green water near the shore, an arrowhead of ducks moved soundlessly. As I watched them, they turned abruptly and scuttled back towards my small wooden dock. Hearing the sputter of a boat, I leaned forward and peered down the lake.

"God, they're at it again!" I picked up my field glasses and scanned the water. A boat full of fishermen loomed up hugely in the binoculars.

"Look at them. The bastards! They're tossing bottles into the water." I paced the room as furiously as if the bottles were being jettisoned into my own living room. "The dump's just down the road!"

Charlie, my dog, pulled the bulk of his golden body up on his haunches and looked at me.

"You know what I'm going to do, Charlie? I'm going to canoe out there and tell them they're breaking the law." I stood for a moment, revelling in the mental images.

I collapsed into the chair. I couldn't do it. As usual, my sense of propriety strong-armed my rebelliousness into submission. The boat with the carousing men disappeared along the shoreline.

"Why do I let them get away with it?" Doing something, anything, couldn't be worse than the fury I felt when I did nothing.

"One of these days, Charlie, I'm not going to be such a pushover."

I sipped my tea, trying to calm myself. As if to bolster my spirits, a fish jumped. Pleasure splashed through me.

When I was a child, I used to spend hours pretending to be a fish. I'd hurl myself out of the lake into the warm air, then let myself crash down into the waiting water and watch a billion pellucid air bubbles explode in front of my open eyes.

"Fish" my parents called me. Later, they would go fishing and smash their catch over the head with the end of a paddle.

Such contradictions baffled me as a child. I'd spent years sorting them out in my analysis with Rudi. Rudi. I couldn't think of her without feeling a softness in my chest. I wondered how she was. My therapist for years, and later on, when that part of my life was over, she'd become an elderly mentor and friend. I missed her. A year ago she'd given in to her daughter's persuasion and gone to live with her in the city. Although I loathed the idea of it, Rudi was aging. Every few weeks I telephoned and with each call, her frailty seemed to increase. As did my anxiety. I still needed her. The last time we had spoken, she had sounded weak and vulnerable. Ever since, I'd felt a vague sense of panic, as if I were out in the middle of a lake on an air mattress that was losing its air.

To this day, I can't eat fish of any kind. When my grandson, Luke, catches one, I always want to put the glistening beauty back in the water where it belongs. But even there, the fish aren't safe. A few years ago, officials put signs along the public wharfs warning people of the level of poison in each species. Those signs made me burn with anger. I cursed the culprits who were polluting the lake and vowed to stop them. But who was there to fight? What was I supposed to do, scream at every motorboat on the lake? Blow up every malfunctioning septic system?

Depressing as it was, I had to accept that the enemy wasn't a person, it was a way of life, as embedded in the culture as gum in a child's hair.

Charlie banged his tail on the table leg and laid his blond head consolingly on my leg. I slid my palm along the velvet smoothness of his forehead. Heavily, I stood up. "Come on, Charlie, we've got Madge this morning."

I confronted the clothes in my closet, considering the various possibilities. Everything felt so staid, so conservative. Who was the person who wore these clothes? Reaching for a forest-green sweat suit I had bought on impulse the week before and not yet worn, I headed for the bathroom.

My face, round as the moon, stared back at me from the mirror. I have always been told I have a kind face, one that engenders trust. But the face that stared back at me this morning had a precarious, doubtful look. The kind that a mother gives her child when she's not sure she's happy with what she sees.

I am losing myself. Like a piece of fruit that's been left out too long, my face is wrinkling and surrendering its shape to the laws of gravity. My jaw, for example, appalls me. Look at the way the skin sags there, drooping from the bone like a wet towel. Jowls are what I can look forward to next.

Only my eyes offer solace. Frog-green with flecks of dark brown, I've always liked my eyes. A client of mine, Norman, said they were "ferocious".

"They go with that name of yours – Jessie Dearborn James. You sound more like a cowgirl than a psychotherapist," Norman had said.

I smiled and began applying face cream. As if the cream were going to do any good.

Positioning my fingers in front of my ears, I pulled my skin tight. A younger, fresher face sprang out from the folds of my own. I bet Madge would have a face lift if she could afford it. She wouldn't have qualms.

I stared at myself unhappily. *What's happening? I don't like my clothes, I don't like my face . . .*

Slowly, as in the fairy story of the Princess and the Pea, I groped under my psychological mattresses for the cause. In terms of career, things were excellent. I was a respected psychotherapist with a waiting list of people who wanted to work with me. It hadn't been easy going back to school, but I had obtained the necessary degree. I was proud of that.

On the home front, things were better than ever with the kids. Ted was managing both his own business and his life as a single parent to Luke. And Robyn was finally home. After being away for over five years, she'd flown in from Sri Lanka a week ago. I had hardly recognized her at the airport. I must have expected her to look older. More mature. But with long dark hair and thin, girlish body, she looked like a teenager. She still wore nothing but black, but now she had a tiny sapphire stud in the side of her nose.

She looks punkish.

Oh, stop. She's home. At last. Maybe now the healing can begin.

The phone rang and I scooted into my office so I could listen to the message as it was delivered to my answering machine. I didn't want to pick it up unless I had to.

"Jessie," the voice hesitated. "It's Officer Tamlin. Jack." He paused, then spoke forcefully as if my machine might put up an argument. "I'm going to cancel my appointment this week. I think I'm all right now. I mean, I'm driving and everything. I don't want to take up any more of your time."

I smiled wryly at his choice of words. Why couldn't he just say he didn't want to come? Why did he have to make it sound like he was concerned about my time?

Jack Tamlin had come a long way. Employed as one of the town's police officers, he'd been in a gruesome car accident a few months ago. His fellow officer had been killed and Jack had almost lost his leg. When Jack recovered and returned to work, he discovered he was unable to drive a car without shaking like a puppy. Embarrassed and ashamed, he had called me. After a few weeks of therapy, he was driving with confidence again. The last time he'd been in, he'd reported that now when he drove, his palms didn't even get sweaty.

"You know how grateful I am," Jack continued into the machine. "I just don't think I need therapy anymore."

I shook my head. For some people, often men, the idea of being in therapy was so threatening, had such a damaging effect on their self-esteem, they only submitted themselves to the process out of dire necessity. These were the ones who showed up late so they wouldn't run into anyone they knew in the waiting room. And they terminated therapy as soon as possible.

"Heaven's be that you might come to therapy because you enjoy it," I said aloud, "because it's gratifying to get to know yourself."

Seeing the light flash on my machine, I flicked back the tape. How had I missed a call? It must have come in late yesterday afternoon. I'd been out until after midnight the night before and hadn't bothered checking the messages until now.

The crisp, cheery voice of the health clinic's receptionist told me to call her back. "Just when you get a moment," she said, obviously trying not to cause alarm.

Drats. They were closed on Wednesday mornings. Now I was going to have to wait until later to find out the results of those tests. But something must be wrong or they wouldn't have phoned.

Feeling unsettled, I went back into the bathroom and faced myself again. I was frowning, so the crease lines around my lips and eyes were even deeper now. There was no doubt about it, a face lift would snug things up nicely.

No.

I hated the idea of giving in to the image makers. Wasn't cosmetic surgery the very antithesis of what I believed in? I, whose profession it was to dig into the realms of truth. Surely that necessitated the honouring of one's various bulges and blotches.

It did. It had to. It was important that people respect their aging process. After all, aging is part of life. I told that to clients all the time, believed it myself and tried to model it.

But there was another part of me that hated the invisibility that came with age: the waiters who didn't notice me, the sales people who served younger people first, the television programs that never showed a person over fifty – except to advertise laxatives. As if older people were just a bunch of sluggish bowels.

"My bowels are just fine," I muttered aloud.

"So are mine, but I don't tell my mirror about it."

I swung around to see Madge standing in the doorway,

her poppy-red mouth moving playfully. "You probably take all that stuff . . ." I said.

Madge shrugged, her grey eyes laughing. "Whatever works. That's what I say – whatever works."

I laced up my running shoes and looked at her. She was wearing purple leotards topped by a hip-length, banana-yellow sweatshirt with the words DO IT on the front in bright red letters. Huge silver hoops hung from her ears.

"You don't have to tell me – I'm bright." Her lips curled mischievously.

"Let's put it this way, you'll never be called a dull, shrivelled-up old lady."

"None of that white-haired, fade-away stuff for me. No way." She blew a gust of air out of her crimson lips. "If I'm going to die, and I haven't decided that I will, I'm going out with a bang, not a whimper."

I chuckled as we headed down the road, Charlie leaping ahead. Madge pumped her arms as she moved into the rhythm of our race walking.

"The only reason I do this," she huffed "is that when I'm ninety, I'll be able to mountain climb with my forty-year-old lover."

Great puffs of air billowed out of my mouth into the cool spring air as I laughed. We settled into a steady, but brisk pace along the country road. Around us the cottages were just visible through the leafless trees. Cottages. Once upon a time they'd been truly that: little cabins in the Muskoka woods for people to escape to. The "escapees" were mostly from Toronto and other southern Ontario towns, but some were Americans, travelling from as far away as Chicago and Pittsburgh and even Baltimore.

In the early days, people nestled their cabins unobtrusively into the woods, painting them bark-brown or coniferous green. And behind each cottage was another structure: the outhouse. Often designed with a half moon cut into the door, these little wooden stalls were fitted with windows that overlooked the lake and stocked with the prerequisite array of Reader's Digests and Dell Crossword Puzzles.

But the affluence of the seventies and eighties had hit Muskoka like a hallucinogenic drug. Suddenly the simplest of cottages burgeoned into an architectural fantasy with guest quarters, laundry facilities and the inevitable Muskoka Room with its handcrafted wooden furniture and glass from floor to ceiling. In these fashion-magazine cottages, washrooms with saunas and hot tubs replaced the old outhouses, which were then torn down or turned into meditation huts.

On the water, boathouses blossomed out onto the lake, boathouses with four or five boat slips, topped with huge sun decks ornamented with yellow umbrellas and designer lawn furniture.

"I'd like to know where these summer people get all their money," Madge said as a truck loaded with lumber rumbled by.

"And these are second homes," I added. "Used a few weeks of the year."

"Crazy," Madge sighed. "But we'd be lost without them. Summer renovations are what feed the locals. For Boyd, they're his bread and butter."

"You mean his champagne and caviar!" Boyd was a contractor renowned for bleeding the summer people like a leech.

"City people should pay city prices – that's what he says."

I couldn't hold myself back. "Just because he's got a license to steal doesn't mean he should use it."

"Come on, all the locals gouge the tourists."

"They jack their prices up – that's different from robbing them."

I didn't want this conversation. I knew it wasn't one I could have cleanly. I didn't like Boyd, although I couldn't say why. It was strange. In my psychotherapy practice, I saw drug addicts, wife beaters, liars and cheats. Yet I always managed to establish an unerring belief in each person's potential redemption. With Boyd, however, I couldn't rally much compassion. And I felt guilty about it.

A lot of people said he'd done a great deal for our community. Just that morning I had read an article in the paper about a development project he'd finished. And Robyn had thought the world of him when he'd been her swim coach in high school. She used to keep a photograph of him on her wall. For years, a blond and boyish Boyd had smiled down on her bed, his white teeth shining.

The photograph had been one that Robyn had taken herself. Once upon a time, she'd been enthralled with photography, sometimes spending hours in the woods with her camera and tripod.

"I saw him again last night," Madge said.

"Oh?" I tried to keep the concern out of my voice. I was nervous about Madge dating Boyd. First of all, there was the age thing – Boyd was in his late thirties, Madge was almost fifty. For her, however, that probably only added to his attraction. But there were other things as well. "Doesn't it bother you that he's married?"

Madge snorted. "Everyone knows he and his wife have separate lives."

"Then why doesn't he separate officially? Instead of trying to cut it both ways?"

"Politics, I guess. Some people don't approve of divorce."

I frowned. Yesterday someone told me they'd seen Boyd at a bar with Donna. Donna was a client of mine that he'd dropped rather brutally a few months before. Did this mean they were seeing each other again?

"The guy's a complete rascal." Madge chuckled. "Obviously very used to getting his own way." She gasped for breath. "I managed to kick him out before he got into my –" she cleared her throat, playing for time – "bed. But it wasn't easy."

I flinched but kept my mouth shut.

"I must admit," Madge went on, "it's awfully nice having a man around again."

"It's nice having certain men around," I wanted to correct. Instead I said, "I don't know which is better, living alone and dealing with the loneliness or being with someone and having to deal with all their hangups."

Madge elbowed me. "You forget the delights."

"You forget the hassles!"

"It's been six months since Ed moved out. And we weren't doing diddly squat at the end there. That's long enough for me to do without sex."

"Six months? Try six years!"

Madge hooted. "I can't."

I thought about Ed's narrow eyes and the way they used to wander over my breasts when he didn't think I would notice.

"The one good thing about menopause," Madge said, "is that, for once in my life, I don't have to worry about birth control."

"Just all those deadly little diseases," I added, unable to stop myself.

Madge groaned. "Here I am, finally free to have free sex and it's not free anymore."

"If it ever was . . ." *Oh, Jessie, don't be such a prude.*

We walked faster, neither risking more conversation.

Fifteen minutes later, we reached the outskirts of town. Tea shops and country inns were coming to life again as winter took off its coat of snow and the tourist season approached. The town was large enough to have a movie theatre, a small shopping mall, a swimming pool and bakery, all of which functioned year round. But by May 24th, the annual metamorphosis would be in full swing. Dozens of stores, in business only from May to Labour Day, would open their doors and hang "Welcome Back" signs in their windows to greet the influx of summer people who would soon triple the area's population.

In the summer the town took on an almost European flavour with art exhibitions in the park, antique boat shows and a parade of tee-shirts emblazoned with LONDON, NEW YORK, MUSKOKA. Artists, painters, potters, glass blowers, quilt makers and silversmiths stocked the craft stores with their wares. For those brief, few months, the movie theatre showed films I actually wanted to see.

I liked the fact that the town had seasons. Like an undergarment, the winter population gave the town its supportive foundation, but it was the summer crowd that dressed it up with flamboyant fashions and startling colours, giving it life and sophistication. The summer people were, after all, on holiday and committed to having a good time. And the town, despite the occasional grumble about the annual invasion, was just as committed to providing it.

The cottagers were offered every opportunity to spend their money. And spend they did. They bought liquor by the case, loading the clinking boxes into mahogany launches that waited at docks built for their convenience. They bought corkscrews with fish heads, raccoon oven mitts and pine-scented toilet paper. They consumed thousands of cones of frozen yogurt, as they acquired hundreds of neon-coloured sail boards and dozens of jet skis. After their buying expeditions, they refreshed themselves in one of the waterside cafes which offered cold beer and jazz.

Muskoka became the playground of Ontario, and cottage property prices, as if wanting to be part of the fun, shot up like fireworks over the bay on the first of July.

"How's it going with the kids? Ted still doing all right?" Madge asked. "You've got to admire him, eh? Ever hear from Luke's mother?"

I shook my head. "Not since the day she propped the note on the washing machine saying she was leaving. Luke was what, five months then?"

"Strange – women are so different now. No matter how bad things were with Ed, when the kids were young, I never could have walked out."

I had liked Luke's mom and wished she could have stayed. "That poor woman, she didn't have a clue who she was or what she wanted. It's hard to give to others when your own barrel is empty." I knew all about that one. So I understood. Besides, I was grateful to have a grandson.

"How old's Luke now? Eight?"

I nodded. "I'm taking him to a powwow in a few weeks. Want to come?"

"A powwow? Isn't that something out of the movies? Like when the natives meet and decide whether or not to go to war?"

"Maybe on television. This one's on the reserve down in Orillia. I don't know much about it, only that they dress up and do ceremonial dances. I've got Luke for the day and thought he might like it."

"You know me, I'm always good for something different. Count me in – unless Boydie-boy wants me."

Anger lurched into my throat at my second place position, but I said nothing.

"Speaking of different," Madge said. "What's it like having Robyn back? She doing ok?"

I swallowed my resentment and carried on. "Hard to tell. If I ask her anything, I get that invaded look. If I don't ask, I don't know." I made myself breathe out the tension in my neck. "Meanwhile she's leaving her laundry everywhere. I feel like I'm living with a teenager again, not a twenty-two year old woman."

"Kids! My son still brings me his sweaters to wash. I never taught him how to do it because I thought his wife would do it when he got married. I tell that to Jeremy, John's current lover, and we all get a good chuckle out of it."

"It's crazy. I couldn't wait to have her back and now I can hardly stand it." A soggy wetness gathered in my chest. "She just seems so angry all the time." *And here you are, a psychotherapist and you can't understand your own daughter.* "Maybe I shouldn't have sold the house."

"Hey, hold your horses. Things change. She can't expect to be away all those years and have you run that huge old house alone. You did write and tell her you were moving. It's not your fault that she was all over the place and didn't get her mail."

"I guess she had to go where the work was," I heard myself say, even though I knew this was a poor explanation.

"What exactly did she do over there for all those years?"

"It sounds awful, but I don't really know. She didn't write much and when she did, they were just postcards. I know she was a mother's helper a few times. And she worked doing children's programs at resorts."

"Whatever. But it's not as if you didn't have a place for her to stay when she finally decided to come back."

"That's the reason I bought the house I did. With the basement room, the kids can visit and I can carry on with clients." My breath was coming in short, anxious bursts. "God, I sound defensive."

"You don't have to defend yourself with me." Madge swatted the air. "Kids always want their parents to stay the same. But life goes on."

I slowed my pace so I could catch my breath. "I guess it's hard for Robyn. When she left, her father was still alive and I was still a frumpy, old housewife, ever willing to do what the family wanted."

"And what does Robyn find when she comes back?" Madge chuckled. "A powerhouse of a mother who's making a damned good life for herself."

"Having a therapist for a mother must be Robyn's

worst nightmare."

"Remember, she's the one who left," Madge reminded me. "Speaking of nightmares, I had a dream about you the other night. You're the dream lady, want to hear it?"

"I'd love to."

"I'm not sure I remember it all, but some Indian was packing up your things. As if you were moving away. Weird, eh?"

I nodded and speculated about what the Indian might symbolize. Going back to nature? Being more in touch with instincts? Was some primal part of me going to send me off in some new direction?

"The natives are getting restless," I heard myself say.

"You're not thinking about moving, are you?"

"Not that I know of."

"You're so unsettled lately . . . "

"I know – I'm putting it down to menopause."

"As long as you're not going anywhere."

"No," I answered, wishing I could share her relief. I knew that even when people lived right beside each other, emotional changes could create distances as wide as oceans.

"Hey! A craft fair!" Madge jogged across the street. I followed reluctantly. I didn't like to stop once we'd started moving, but I'd never been able to hold back Madge from a fair.

In the little park a dozen craft tables were set up, displaying hand-painted shirts, pottery, blown glass and other craft items. While Madge went over to look at some basket weaving, I wove my way through the clumps of people.

Feeling someone's eyes on me, I turned. A man's face

met mine, a full-lipped, dark-skinned face that held itself openly towards me. His eyes pulled away from mine and returned to the drawing he was etching on some leather. He drew freehand, effortlessly, as if the design were already in the leather and all he had to do was trace it out.

Fascinated, I watched the way his hands worked the leather, touching it in a way that made it an intimate act. Sensing my gaze, he glanced up and smiled. His black eyes entered mine. Heat stung my face.

"Breathe!" a voice hissed.

Madge! I half turned, grinned.

"Nice stuff, eh?"

"His work is beautiful."

"I wasn't admiring his work," Madge chortled. "I don't think you were either."

I elbowed Madge, but she carried on.

"Look at that hair!"

As Madge spoke, the man turned and I caught a glimpse of the resplendent black rope of it, as thick as a horsetail and just as long. A thong of leather interlaced with some forest green beads and two feathers held it in place.

I imagined loosening the strands, letting them slither over my bare body as he lay on top of me, his smooth skin sliding against mine.

Get a grip, woman. But my imagination was off and running. My body felt like a jungle full of gazelles pressing against the walls of my skin.

"He's luscious," Madge continued. "A bit young for you, but lots of women are going with younger men. Sexually, it makes far more sense, don't you think?"

This time, I dug my elbow home, and hard, too.

Madge stopped talking, but the smile remained on her mouth.

I crossed my arms in front of my chest. What was all this about? The fervour of my response to this man was outrageous. Over the last few years, the sexual side of me had sort of slipped into sleep. But this man was shaking me awake. I yanked my eyes away.

"Look," Madge said. "He's sketching little trees into the leather."

Stretching forward, I could see a line of lone pine trees etched into the belt he was working on. I ran my fingers along the length of one of the finished belts and turned it over. There, burned into the leather, was his name: Harley Skinkeeper. The name was familiar and unfamiliar all at the same time. What was going on here? I pulled at Madge.

"Come on. Let's get out of here." Without waiting for her, I turned and started into a light jog. Charlie lopped beside me.

"Well, that was interesting" Madge commented when we were back on our way, heading towards the lake.

I wanted to say something, but no words came. I felt too embarrassed to talk. What was the matter with me? Surely at my age I was past such shenanigans. I quickened my pace and was grateful when I could smell the trees. I looked up and saw the park only a few hundred yards ahead. Instinctively, both of us slowed our pace and became quiet. I felt my breath deepen and my body calm as we moved among the tree trunks.

Although there were several hundred trees in the whole park, in the central area, a few dozen had been allowed to grow to their full magnificence. Their massive girths thundered out of the ground and thrust into the air with incredible power.

I looked up. Above me the branches arched towards each other, forming a sanctuary of stillness. Pale, white swords of light pierced through from the sky, illuminating the orange-red pine needles that covered the forest floor. I took a deep breath and the thick, rich smell of tree bark and rotting leaves went streaking into my lungs.

"It's funny how things change," reflected Madge. "When you first brought me here as a child, this forest scared me. Imagine. It felt so wild."

Walking beside Madge, I let my hands stroke each passing tree. To me, these woods had only ever been a refuge. They settled me, took me beneath the conflicts of my life to a place of strength and solidity. No, these trees had only ever been my mentors. They were the peace keepers.

"Then you introduced me to all those tree games," Madge said. "What were we then, seven or eight years-old?"

There had been a hundred games. Games for rainy days, games for sunny days, adventure games, quiet games, as many games as there were hours to play in. All involving trees.

This had been the enchanted forest, where the fairy tale of the trees lived and breathed. The opening ritual had always been the same and early on, I had appointed myself the one to begin it: I led, showing Madge and my sister and brother how to open their palms and stroke each tree trunk in a slow gesture of greeting. This was the magic signal that told the trees that kindred spirits were now amongst them. We called ourselves the "tree people", and considered ourselves a special species, born to look like ordinary human beings, but inside, sap ran thickly through our veins.

The trees recognized us and once we had each brushed our open palms along their trunks, they awakened, as if from a spell. To communicate with a particular tree, we lay on the ground, our small heads touching the trunk as our eyes scaled its impressive reach into the sky. Attuned in this way, we soon discovered that a tree could transfer its thoughts into our bodies without a sound.

Almost always, the first thing a tree told us was its name. Sometimes we had to wait to hear it, but no one would speak until all of us had received the tree's communication. Then, after counting to three, we would all say the name the tree had told us at the same time. Nearly always, at least two of us would say the same name.

The huge evergreen with the plume soaring up into the belly of the clouds, told us its name was Skybrusher. With its giant bristles, it could brush the clouds wherever it wanted, sweeping them away to leave the sky clean and blue again. We often asked it to clear away thunder clouds when we were planning picnics, and it always did.

The two trees with their trunks pressed solidly together were called The Lovers. As a child, Madge had been fascinated with those two trees and the way their branches intertwined. Once she pointed to some sap oozing down one of the trunks. This was followed by weeks of speculation. Did trees fall in love? Could they have babies? Did they have sex?

As we walked through the grove now, Madge touched a beech tree with a bulbous protrusion erupting out of its side. I smiled. "Remember how I used to think a baby raccoon was living in there, making that bump?"

Madge nodded. "I wasn't much better. I thought it was a beehive. I never got too close in case a bee would come out and sting me."

I reached for the next tree. "And here's Red. Big Red." I looked up into a gigantic maple. In summer, its muscular limbs seemed to ride the wind like a cowboy.

We walked on until we came to my favourite tree: Candelabra. A magnificent pine with a trunk over four feet wide, its torso rose up mightily for about fifteen feet, then split into four offshoots, each rising straight as an arrow, a tree in its own right. The most remarkable part was that just as the gargantuan trunk divided, there was a little bowl-like sitting place. As children, it had taken all of us together, one standing on top of the other's shoulders, to hoist one of us up there, but oh, the bliss of sitting in this tree's giant palm.

Looking at it now, the sitting place seemed unreachable. How did I ever climb up there the night of the rape? I guess when you feel crazy, you can do crazy things.

I leaned back against a tree and breathed deeply. I didn't want to remember that night now. I let my back fall against the solidity of the trunk and felt calm. "Strange how the older I get, the simpler are my pleasures," I said.

Madge chewed her lower lip. "I'm the opposite. The older I get, the harder it is to find what I want."

"What do you want?"

"Right now? Boyd."

I nodded thoughtfully. Over and over in my psychotherapy work, I saw how people wanted things that couldn't possibly fulfil them. Strange how you can't get enough of what you don't really want.

Madge nudged my arm and we wandered down to the lake. A strong wind breezed across the water, cooling my sweaty skin. The surface of the lake was choppy as if being pushed in too many different directions.

"Isn't that Elfreda Pepper over there?" Madge asked, looking down the shore.

Following Madge's glance, I saw a small-bodied old woman walking unsteadily between the trees. My back tightened.

"There's someone I wish you could work with." Madge said, looking at me intently.

I said nothing. I made sure my face gave away nothing. Elfreda had called me once, but she'd been drinking, so we hadn't been able to get very far. It was difficult being a psychotherapist in a small town. In a big city, the lives of clients and therapist seldom interfaced. But in a small community, the boundaries were more difficult to maintain and I was always encountering clients: at the supermarket, at garage sales and social events. Once I'd sat with a client trying to dismantle a debilitating depression, only to be introduced to him an hour later at a dinner party.

"Imagine what that old woman's been through." Madge sighed deeply. "Nursing a husband through cancer and then having him and her daughter die in the same month. Cancer and a car crash. What a load. No wonder she wants to drink herself into oblivion." She dipped her sweat band in the cold water and wrung it out.

"Humbling, isn't it, what people have to bear," I said quietly. Bone breaking abuse, life-guzzling addictions, death of loved ones. No one was exempt from the egregious cruelties of life. I knew. I heard about them day after day in my counselling work.

"Did I ever tell you about seeing her sleeping down here?" Madge continued. "She was curled up under a tree! Just like a bag lady. It was pathetic."

I shook my head sadly. I didn't know Elfreda well, but from what I'd heard, the woman was exceptional, when sober. She'd championed the opening of a women's shelter in town, set up a food bank, raised money for needy children. Before the tragedy in her family, she'd organized some of the interesting old ladies in town for outings, discussions and social reform. They called themselves The Granny Group. Over the winter, I had led them in an exercise class once a week, although Elfreda hadn't been there in a while. When she was, she had the quickest wit of them all.

"I just hate to see such a fine old lady go down the tube like that. Isn't there anything you can do?" urged Madge.

"I wish. But my mother's alcoholism taught me well. You can lead a horse away from water, but you can't force it not to drink."

Madge adjusted the orange sweat band around her forehead. "Well," she said unhappily, "we'd better push off."

We turned to walk back through the trees.

"What the hell is – "

"Going on," I whispered. I tried to swallow but my throat was dry. Pickup trucks were parked out by the road and men were cordoning off an area around several of the big trees. Two men in hard hats and steel-toed boots were standing beside Skybrusher. A chain saw was at their feet.

Chapter 2

Surely in God's name, they're not –" My voice died in my throat, along with my hope. Numbly, I watched as one of the men walked around the circumference of the tree calculating its width.

"They are!"

Madge's words sounded far away as if I'd already begun running across the park. I saw my hand raise involuntarily in some feeble attempt to stop her words from coming towards me.

In front of me the air lightened as if I were standing on the edge of an abyss. My legs itched with an impulse to run away before something dangerous happened. Because something dangerous was close to happening. Very close.

I watched the man lift the chain saw, heard the engine explode into a hard, biting sound and felt Madge grab my arm. A sick dizziness came over me. My legs quivered, caught between running towards the men and running away. Then a great gust of energy thumped against my back and swept me forward.

As terrifying as it was to feel myself careening through space towards these men, a great relieving emancipation swept over me. I was no longer holding myself back, no longer enduring the outrage of complacency. In a frenzy of exhilaration, I flung myself over the yellow tape barrier, my body demanding to be reckoned with.

The man holding the saw jabbed at a switch and the machine stopped. The two men stared at me as they might a rabid dog.

"What's going on here?" I tried to make my voice sound authoritative, but calm.

There were two men. One was round-bellied and compacted and looked as if he'd been stuffed into clothes that were far too small for him. The other man was thin with a face as closed off as a boarded-up house.

"We've been hired by the owner of this property to take down these trees. . . " said the thick-bodied man. He rolled his eyes. They looked as hard as bowling balls. "So the construction – "

"Construction? What construction?" someone called. I looked up and saw that a crowd was gathering around us.

"I thought this park belonged to the town," I said, ignoring the panic that was fluttering in my belly.

"All I know is we're to take these down. There's six condos going in here."

"How come we never heard about it?" another voice shouted from the crowd.

The heavy man's face became red and dark like a bruise. He looked down at his saw. "We're not here to talk about it. We're here to do it."

I stared at him disbelievingly. Refusing to look at me, he leaned over and yanked the cord of the machine. The saw burst into a hard, metallic whine. In a frighteningly abrupt movement, he swung the buzzing saw against the tree.

I flung my body against the trunk, inches from the bite of the saw.

"Curt, stop!" the thin man shouted.

Stubbornly, Curt gnashed the saw into the tree, cutting the wood just inches from my body. Wood chips spit into my face.

I saw people's mouths open to scream. Feeling faint, I closed my eyes.

Get out of here, Jessie. Now!

The sound of the saw was so horrible I wanted to cover my ears, but I was too terrified to move. I pushed my back into the tree, feeling its strength and stillness against my spine. Beneath me my feet burrowed into the ground like roots. When I opened my eyes, I saw Madge, as if in slow motion, bounding forward and grabbing Curt's shoulders. Thrown off balance, he dropped the saw. The engine spluttered and quiet shot through the air.

"Bitches!" Curt spat.

Charlie growled at him and moved his body against mine.

Eying the dog, the other man said, "What we're doing is legal."

"It might be legal, but it isn't right," a strong male voice said in a low but commanding tone.

I followed the voice to a man in the crowd. Harley. It was Harley who had spoken. Wearing a wide-brimmed leather hat, he was standing beside a bicycle. Despite the seriousness of the moment, I grinned at him. A wry smile crossed his mouth.

"Legal is enough." Turning to me, Curt added, "Now, are you going to be a nice lady and move, or am I going to call the cops and tell them how crazy you are?"

Wordless as a tree, I stood. Beside me, Madge widened her stance and crossed her arms.

Curt scowled. "I'm going to get the cops." He strode from the park.

People rushed towards us, all talking at once. Some patted me on the back, others twittered with disapproval.

"You just about got yourself sliced." Harley looked at me with wide, appraising eyes.

"Thanks to Madge," I said. Feeling weak, I put my arm around Madge's shoulder to prop myself up.

"Teach'em to mess with the likes of us," Madge boasted, laughing nervously.

Harley's eyes roamed solemnly through the boughs above him. "Too bad. Some of these must be over a hundred years old. Real elders."

I looked at him hard. "It's not over yet."

He raised an eyebrow. "The way I figure it, the cops will be here in five minutes and the trees will be down in ten."

"And you'll be in jail in fifteen," Madge said to me, pouncing in right after him. "For obstructing or some other thing they'll dream up." She moved from one foot to the other. "Look, I don't know about you, but I don't fancy the idea of going to jail. I think we should get out of here while the getting's good. We've made our point." She shrugged. "You know what they say, 'You can't fight City Hall'."

I stared at Madge, but she wouldn't meet my eyes. How could she say this? I looked over at Harley, expecting him to be dealing with his own inner turmoil as well, but his eyes reached out to me. He nodded as if responding to some question he saw in my face.

As we talked, a police car pulled up over by the road. "I wish I had something to tie myself in with," I said. "Something strong like a leash or –"

"Will this do?" Harley handed me his bike chain.

"Yes!" Quickly, I wrapped the heavy chain around the girth of the tree and locked myself in. Beside us, Madge groaned. When I looked up, Curt was trudging towards me, a police officer in tow.

"That's the one," Curt pointed at me.

"Jessie!"

"Officer Tamlin." The officer and I looked at each other warmly.

Leaning towards me, he whispered, "Left you a message. Did you get it?"

I nodded and smiled. Being a therapist in a small town was very interesting sometimes.

Satisfied, he stood back. "Geez, Jessie, they told me it was some lunatic." He surveyed the crowd, nodding at some of the people he knew. Adjusting to the official circumstances, he cleared his throat and said more formally, "Now, look, Mrs James, I know you and some folks here have different ideas about these trees being cut down, but they are on private property. And that means the owner has the right to do whatever he wants with them, whether we like it or not." He took off his cap and scratched his head. "I'm going to have to ask you to move."

My face flushed. People in the crowd stared, waiting to see what I was going to do. Some moved back a little as if expecting me to rush away. But my body stayed where it was.

The crowd, which was even bigger now, became agitated.

"It's criminal to kill these trees," someone shouted.

"It's not right. We want a hearing."

"A public inquiry."

"Nobody's got the right to kill trees."

One gravelly voice called out over the others. "It's an election year, Jack. Don't forget that. The mayor won't like it if you blow this election for him." My eyes jumped from Tamlin's grimacing face to the person who had spoken. Elfreda's chuckles skipped through the crowd.

Madge elbowed me. In a strong voice, she said, "The mayor won't want bad publicity just before an election."

I followed along, right on cue, and said loudly, "I think we should get in touch with the press. They might be very interested in this story."

Madge arched her finely pencilled eyebrows. "Yes. Absolutely."

"For Chrissakes," Curt groaned. "Let's get the buggers down before these crackpots blow this into World War Three."

Officer Tamlin gripped his night stick. "Hold on, everybody. Just hold on. I'm going to talk to the mayor." Pulling himself tall, he walked out of the park towards the government offices.

"Christ!" Curt turned away.

"I'm going to call my lawyer," Madge said. "Find out your rights."

"My rights? Don't you mean *our* rights?"

Madge waved away my concern. "Whatever . . ."

"My phone's closest," I told her. "And while you're there, could you call Dr. Andrews and cancel?" Since I had a tricky dental procedure planned for that afternoon, I hadn't booked any clients. "And, you'd better take Charlie back."

Madge nodded. "Some people will do anything to get

out of going to the dentist." She pecked my cheek lightly and gave a sidelong glance towards Harley. "I know you're in good hands." Grinning, she made her way through the crowd.

Embarrassed that Harley might have heard her, I leaned back against the tree and closed my eyes.

As I waited, people gathered around me to talk and give their advice about what should be done. I saw someone push through the crowd.

"Mother! What are you doing?"

Robyn's thin, bird-like body stood rigidly beside me. Dressed in black jeans and tee-shirt, she shoved her thin hands into her pockets. Her delicate skin looked very white. I sighed. Why did she have to show up now?

"What does it look like I'm doing?"

She looked at me sullenly. "Making a fool of yourself?"

I made myself breathe. Time to call on my therapeutic skills.

"I'm embarrassing you, am I?" Seeing Robyn's eyes widen, I took the challenging tone out of my voice and tried to explain. "They're trying to cut these trees down, Robyn. I've known these trees since I was little. I -"

"Can't you write a letter or something?" She stared at the chain around my waist. "Do something less ridiculous?"

My spirits deflated, but something in me rallied. "Maybe it's time for someone to look ridiculous. Maybe if more people were willing to look ridiculous, the world would be a better place. With more trees!"

"Mother, you're ranting. People will think you're c– " She stopped herself.

Crazy.

"People will think you're courageous," Harley cut in. "They'll see you as a woman with enough guts to do what's right." His voice was soft, but firm.

Robyn narrowed her eyes. Realizing that people were listening, she turned abruptly, so abruptly that her hair spun out behind her almost hitting me in the face. Stiffly, she strode away.

Overwhelmed, I slumped against the tree. When I opened my eyes a moment later, I saw Tamlin at the edge of the park, heading resolutely towards me.

"The pace doesn't let up, does it?" Harley said, an amused smile lifting the corner of his wide mouth.

I straightened my body to armour myself for what was to come.

"At least he didn't bring reinforcements," Harley said, standing close. "I had twenty after me once."

"Clear the area," Tamlin called, making big sweeping motions with his hands towards the crowd. "I want everyone out of here. And I mean everyone." As people in the crowd grumbled, he put his hands on his hips, revealing his billy club. "The mayor's decided to look into the matter, so you can all go home and relax." He began herding people away.

Reluctantly, the crowd dispersed. Some waved as they left. Elfreda stood unwaveringly in the midst of the milling crowd. Smiling crookedly, she shot her arm out and lifted her thumb in victory. Tamlin hurried over to escort her off the grounds.

Harley scowled. "Sure the mayor will look into it. Right after the trees are down. These guys must think we're slow learners." He passed me a piece of paper. "It's the combination to the lock. Just in case."

"And you, Mrs. James," Tamlin said, striding towards me. "Leave this to the mayor. Let him take care of it. That's what he's elected to do." When I didn't respond, he added, "I'll give you some time to think it over." Then, quietly, he added, "Don't make me arrest you, because if I have to, I will. It's my job." He turned to Harley. "You better move on there, mister."

Harley gave a small, almost imperceptible nod to Tamlin, who moved off to attend to the last few stragglers. Raising one long, curved thigh, he moved astride his bicycle. For a moment, he surveyed me. "You're some woman," he said and rode off.

Chapter 3

When everyone had gone, I slid to the ground. I felt exhilarated and exhausted all at the same time. What had I done?

Feeling dazed, I watched people strolling along the sidewalk at the periphery of the park. Did these people have any idea of what had just happened here? Some looked oblivious, others stared at me curiously. What had they heard? That some crazy old lady had tied herself to a tree? I flinched.

I must look like some card-carrying member of the lunatic fringe! Crazy old lady. Crazy old lady, they'll whisper as I walk down the street.

Normally, I take my respectability for granted. My clients and friends treat me as a person of integrity. Now, however, sitting alone, chained to this tree, the memory of Robyn's words stung me. I probably did look ridiculous.

It would be worth being called names if I could save the trees. But soon, Tamlin would return to arrest me and my beloved trees were going to come crashing down. Forces much more powerful than my good intentions were obviously in gear here.

So get out. Get away. While you still can.

I rested against the tree and tried to think. Tiredness

pulled me into sleep and after a while, I jerked awake. At the edge of the park, a woman hurried by, pushing a baby in a pram with one hand and holding on to a preschooler in the other. The woman was frowning and I could hear whispers between her and the older child. It was starting. Humiliation swept through me.

The child had some sort of costume on and I remembered seeing somewhere a notice for a spring pageant. Yanking herself free, the child bounded towards me, stopping dead in her tracks in front of me. Her little homemade cellophane wings trembled uncertainly on the paper chest band that held them to her body. On the wings were blobs of sun yellow and jello orange, obviously her own work.

The child was supposed to be a butterfly, but with her cherubic face and big, believer eyes, she looked more like an angel. Uncertainly her tongue wet her lips and she caught her lower one in her teeth. Her fear was palpable, yet she held her ground.

"It's all right," I said gently. "I won't hurt you."

"Mommy says you're gonna save the trees being chopped."

I looked into the little girl's face. It was as open as the future. "I'm going to try."

She clapped her hands together gleefully, threw her head back and looked up. We were so close that I could see the reflection of the trees in her eyes.

Then, her mission complete, the girl skipped back to her mother, wings flapping. At the edge of the park, she turned and waved exuberantly, as if saying goodbye to her very best friend. Thoughtfully, the mother raised her hand and waved as well.

"Starting a fan club?"

"Madge! Where have you been? I thought. . ." My eyes sought Madge's to reestablish the camaraderie of a few hours ago, but Madge was studying her fingernails.

"Got Smedly," she reported matter-of-factly. "Finally. He says you don't have a leg to stand on. Legally, anyway." She bit at a nail.

I searched Madge's face. Something wasn't right.

"You're not going to believe this," Madge said flatly, still not looking at me.

"Believe what?"

"Who owns this land. Who's developing it . . ."

Madge's glance finally swung towards me and our eyes locked. For a moment, neither of us spoke.

"Boyd!"

Madge grinned. Then, as if remembering something, the smile faded. "I went to see him. He definitely wants you out of here." She snickered. "Which is putting it mildly." Making her lips like the knot on the end of a balloon, she filled her mouth with air so her cheeks bulged. Then she blew the air out noisily. "He wanted you arrested right away, but I asked him to wait." She looked at me, and seeing no reaction, carried on. "He wants to settle this peacefully."

I frowned. There was an uncomfortable twitch in my stomach.

Madge rolled her eyes at my doubt. "This is his land, you know. He did buy it." She looked away from me. "He showed me the plans for the condominiums. They're not so bad. He's only going to take down the trees he has to. The minimum."

"The minimum! How can you support him killing

any of them? We've known these trees all our lives." I stared at Madge incredulously. "You're a tree person, too." I wanted to shake her, wake her out of her trance.

She dropped her hands to her sides. "I don't like this. You don't like this, but, believe it or not, Boyd isn't thrilled about taking these trees down either. However, as he says, you can't make an omelette without breaking eggs. And he's promised me he's going to plant more. In fact, he even offered to let you organize the landscaping."

My fury sizzled. "Come on! Co-opt the opposition. That's the oldest trick in the book. He must think I'm an idiot." The red heat in my stomach rose up and spewed into words. "You tell Boyd to go screw himself – if you're not doing that for him already."

Madge's slap was sharp and painful, but nothing compared to the anguish I was feeling inside. We looked at each other with astonished repentance, then fell into each other's arms.

"I deserved that," I said, my voice low.

"No, I shouldn't have."

I tried to explain. "I'm on totally new ground here. I want to stand up for what I believe in, but it's so hard..."

Madge was suddenly optimistic. "Look, how about we unchain you and I take you out for dinner? We'll brainstorm possibilities. There must be some other way to put the brakes on this thing."

The thick, spicy smell of garlic linguine filled my nose. We'd go to Giorgio's. I'd sit in one of those sumptuous wing-back chairs. Over a long drink, we'd come up with another plan.

"I need to stay here."

"Jessie, there's nothing more you can do."

"You may be right. But I have to stay until the end of it. I wouldn't feel good otherwise."

Madge stared at me as if she were seeing me for the first time. After a while, she nodded and said, "You sure you don't want me to send Smedly over?"

I shook my head. Lawyers helped people with their legal rights. I had no legal rights.

The two of us stood awkwardly, neither speaking. Finally she said, "Well, I guess I'd better be off. I have a thousand things I need to do today." Her voice was brittle with brightness. "I'll come by later and see how you're doing." She turned reluctantly. At the edge of the park she called, "Good luck!" Then, as if to make up for her abandonment, she blew me a kiss.

Resentfully, I watched her go. Why couldn't she have stayed and fought it out with me? She'd grown up with these trees too. Suddenly the burden of what I was doing weighed down on me. It wasn't fair. If Madge didn't care, why should I?

Go home. Before you get yourself in worse trouble.

Left alone, my thoughts pushed each other around. Despite the free-for-all going on in my head, my body settled itself resolutely against the tree. Although it didn't make sense to me, my body seemed to know something, seemed to have some wisdom that was navigating me through the slums of my thinking to some inner path of rightness. My instinct told me that if I abandoned this knowing, all would be lost.

You'd be proud of me, Rudi. You always told me to trust my body and here I am doing it.

I smiled, thinking back on my time in therapy. "Move out of the smaller knowing into the bigger knowing," she used to tell me. I now knew fully what she had meant.

I was staying. Straining against the chain, I scanned the park for Tamlin but could see no sign of him. I relaxed back against the tree. He was going to show up when he was going to show up. There was no point in anticipating him.

As if celebrating my decision, the evening sky flared up with pink and yellow streamers that paraded from one end of the horizon to the other. Through a clearing in the trees, I saw the colours of the sunset darken, deepening into streaks of red and purple so intense I was awestruck by the beauty of it. Even the boughs of the trees seemed to stretch up into a party of colour.

One by one in the cerulean blue sky, tiny stars began to flicker until it looked as though there were a thousand fairies up there, each holding a tiny sparkler. I felt a deep pleasure in my belly.

My whole body pulsed with the wonder of it. I felt the blood flooding through my veins and became aware of my skin and how it contained me, as a leather bag might hold a scoop of fish and water from a stream. For a moment, my skin softened, became permeable and the boundary of myself dissolved. Then a realization came to me – that although the physicalness of my body made me feel separate from the nature around me, my body and the earth's body were really the same thing. In actuality, I was nothing more or less than the earth in a smaller package. That meant that the earth's survival and my survival were one and the same.

Standing up for these trees was not only a statement about them and their right to survive, it was an affirmation of all life, my own included. The destruction had to stop and I had to be a part of insisting that it stop, even if the only listeners were myself and the earth itself.

As I sat pondering these thoughts in the dimming light, I saw someone approaching. Tamlin? No, this person was small, with skinny legs, and was carrying a bundle. The bundle was dropped at my feet, revealing the person behind it.

"Elfreda."

"Thought you might need these," the old woman said, her voice slightly slurred. There, in a heap, was a flashlight, sleeping bag, thermos, a sandwich wrapped in cellophane and a few books. "Just mystery stuff. Didn't think you'd want anything literary."

"No, this is definitely an occasion for light reading," I replied, slipping into my therapist mode. "Pull up a tree."

Elfreda glanced at me warily, but crouched down. Close now, I realized how small the woman was, almost gnome-like in form. She was wearing a Toronto Blue Jays cap turned sideways on her head and a rumpled jacket. The laces of both running shoes were undone.

"From what I hear, you've been having a rough time…" I ventured.

Elfreda shut her eyes. For a moment, I wondered if the old lady had fallen asleep. But when she opened her eyes, they were almost pleading. "Don't!"

Startled, I softened my voice. "Don't what?"

Elfreda scowled as if I were purposely misunderstanding her. "Don't do your therapist number. Don't pretend to understand when you don't." She shook her head resolutely. "Have you lost a child? Have you had a child killed? Have you?" There was spittle at the side of her mouth.

I sighed, wishing I hadn't opened the conversation like this. Obviously, Elfreda needed therapy and this was no time to start it. I answered as I would have answered anybody. "No. But I've had my own suffering. And when I've suffered, it's helped me to talk it through. Sometimes talking helps people feel better."

"I don't give a dog's diddle about feeling better."

Great, I thought. What a lovely way to spend an evening, chained to a tree alongside a hostile old woman.

"Everyone's treating me like a bloody basket case," Elfreda complained.

Words leapt into my throat, but I held them back. Then I decided to let them go. If Elfreda wanted straight talk, she could have straight talk. "If you want people to stop treating you like a basket case, stop acting like one."

A smile slowly bloomed on her face at my directness. "I just might, one day. If I can find something worth doing it for." She cast her glance up into the trees like a child throws a beach ball. "Being here, among these trees, is the only time I don't feel crazy."

"They've bailed me out a few times too," I said quietly.

Elfreda looked at me with interest. She nodded as if acknowledging the pain she heard in my voice. For a few moments we sat quietly, like any two women might, sitting with our suffering.

"Did you know there's a sitting place half way up that tree there?" I gestured towards Candelabra. "Not easy to get to, but wonderful."

"You don't say!" When her eyes found the spot, she grinned. For a second her face lost its jigsaw puzzle of lines and became a picture of aged wisdom. "Sometimes when I can't sleep I come and lie out here. I know it sounds stupid, but these trees are my friends."

I nodded. I understood.

A thought pulled at Elfreda's smile and soon the lines appeared again, tangling her skin into a knot of unhappiness. "But I always get hassled."

"After my husband died, I couldn't sleep for weeks," I said. "It's awful at the beginning. I know. Everything reminded me of him."

My words seemed to settle her. Again, we sat silently and looked at the trees.

"What'll you do when the cops come?" she asked.

"I don't know."

"Tamlin won't come till morning. But he'll come early. At first light. At least, that's what he did when I used to sleep out here. Get me out of sight before people started moving around."

"I think he's hoping that if he gives me enough time to think about it, I'll change my mind and go home."

"Will you?"

"No."

A small smile skimmed over the old woman's lips, but her eyes spoke a warning. "They've got the power on their side, you know. Once they have you out of the way, those men will be back with their saws and that will be the end of it."

I dropped my face into my open palms. I was tired, very tired. "Yes and I'll be in jail. Unless you can think of something else I can do – I'm out of ideas myself."

Elfreda's body slumped forward. She closed her eyes and the shadows made her face look deeply furrowed. Her chest rose and fell in an erratic, agitated way. Finally, in a voice so quiet I could barely hear it, she spoke.

"It's the pain that I can't stand." Her eyes were open now and full of jagged hurt. "The pain of things . . . being destroyed." Her eyes clawed at mine. "How do you stand it?"

I took a big breath. It was an important question, one I'd spent a lot of time thinking about. As a psychotherapist, I'd seen people endure staggering sorrows. The amount of pain some people faced was truly daunting. It was my job to try and help them handle the pain. During my years of work, I'd learned that everyone had their own way of coping: some marched courageously into the feelings, sweating it out; some tried to distract themselves; others numbed themselves out with drink or drugs or sex, until it was over. Everyone had their own way of surviving. So, as much as I wanted to offer Elfreda a profundity about pain, I couldn't.

"I guess I've learned to wait it out," I said finally. "Pain doesn't go on forever. I was just thinking about that a minute ago – how even though there's the awfulness of these trees being threatened, the sunset still happens. And it's still staggeringly beautiful. Life, thank goodness, has a way of insisting on itself. I find if I can get myself to focus on what's beautiful, I have a chance of handling what's painful. Because I want to learn to handle pain. Not just run from it. That's what my mother did – run. She would do anything she could to avoid pain. Including drinking a bottle of gin a day."

Elfreda nodded. "Best anaesthetic I know."

"The problem is, you need to keep pouring it into your body. And it makes most bodies sick."

Elfreda's eyes deadened. Without looking at me, the old woman shook her head and struggled to her feet. I'd lost her.

I looked at her and smiled. I knew there was no point in saying anything more. Psychologically, addictions were world class wrestlers. Until a person learned a lot of tricks about fighting back, they ran the show. "Thanks for what you brought," I called after her as she meandered off into the night. She looked small and vulnerable. Feeling chilled, I unzipped the sleeping bag and crawled down into it.

How I yearned for the comfort of my own bed. It was dark now. *Go. No one will see you. You can be in your own cosy bed within minutes.*

Something sticky was in my hair. Turning on the flashlight, I spotted a thin rope of sap oozing from the cut made earlier by the saw.

I touched the wound with my finger, then pulled it away. This was the finger I had scraped in my skirmish with Curt. I moved my finger into the light. The sap and my own blood joined.

Chapter 4

I woke to blackness. There was a noise, a strange noise. Barking. Not Charlie's resonant, deep-throated barking, but the vicious, snarling yap of an attack dog. Car lights streaked by and a door slammed. This was spooky. Very spooky.

Get out of here. Now!

My hand fumbled with the bicycle lock. Even if I could have remembered the combination, I couldn't see the numbers on the lock. Desperately, I felt around for the flashlight. The snarling grew louder.

Knowing there was no time, I concentrated on listening. There was another sound now. A cold, metallic jingling. It was a menacing sound and not knowing what it was frightened me. Just don't let it have anything to do with snakes. I can handle anything but snakes.

Dog tags! That's what the sound was. Then I heard a dog's breathy panting. Moving closer.

Teeth. Bared, canine teeth were suddenly inches from my face. Snarling. Yapping. I threw up my arms and covered my head, hopelessly trying to protect myself.

"What's the matter, Mrs. James? Don't you like dogs?"

I lowered my arms just enough to see a dark figure standing before me. That voice. Modulated into softness, almost petulant. It was a voice I'd heard many times before. The man stepped closer. The dog's mouth snapped and foamed.

"Get the dog off!" I shouted.

The man pulled the animal back a few inches. Finding the flashlight, I shone it up at the man. From that angle, the light made grotesque shadows on his face.

"Boyd?!"

He bowed dramatically like an actor in a murder mystery. "So, Mrs. James. You going to save these trees?"

I did not speak. Had he been drinking? Fear gripped at my chest, making it hard to breathe.

"Perhaps you don't understand the importance of this project, how many jobs it will create. There will be many unhappy townspeople if this venture is . . . killed. What are a few trees? We can plant more trees."

"That's like saying it's all right to kill people because more can be produced," I said, finding my voice.

Boyd shook his head. "Spoken like a true fanatic." He loosened the leash an inch and I felt the moistness of the dog's breath on my skin. "I know about fanatics. They don't respond to reason. Only power." The dog growled. "Like King here. He knows who's boss. He knows who's expendable. It would be easy enough to explain. I'd simply tell the police I was out walking my dog when we came across some vagrant sleeping illegally on my property. Is it my fault if the dog attacked in order to protect me? That sounds reasonable to me, Mrs. James. Doesn't it sound reasonable to you?"

Breathe, Jessie. Nothing's going to happen. He's trying to scare you.

Yes, but he's been drinking. You know how stupid people get when they've been drinking! If Boyd lets go of that leash for even a second, I'll lose half my face.

I tried to settle myself down. I couldn't believe this was happening. As if it wasn't strange enough for me to be out in the middle of the night defending trees, I had to be fighting off Boyd and his dog. If I didn't have my shaking body to remind me this was real, I would have thought I was in the middle of a bizarre dream. Or nightmare.

The dog jerked his head to the side and burst into a paroxysm of barking. The hair on its neck pointed straight up.

"I smell skunk," Boyd said. He peered into the darkness nervously.

As if out of thin air, Harley appeared.

Boyd yanked the dog to his side for protection. "Another fanatic. Get off my property."

Harley bent down and reached out his hand to the dog. King stopped barking and began wagging his tail. "And who's going to make me, you and this ferocious dog of yours?" King took a friendly step towards Harley.

Boyd snapped the dog's leash so hard the animal was pulled off its feet. "I'll have you arrested."

Harley stood up. "We've done that number, remember?"

"Yes, but you don't learn. How long were you in for last time?" Boyd turned to me. "Did you know this man was a criminal? Convicted of assault?"

I looked at Harley. From the way he treated animals, I doubted Harley could hurt anything unless extremely provoked.

"That's your name for it," Harley said. "To me it was slapping the hand of a greedy man who was trying to take what didn't belong to him." Harley's eyes remained steadily on Boyd. "That girl's still fucked up."

"That girl was always fucked up."

Something flickered in Harley's eyes and Boyd tensed as if expecting Harley to lunge at him. Stuffing his hands in his pockets, Harley turned to me. "I'll be keeping an eye out," he said, then held out something to the dog who lurched forward and devoured it before Boyd could restrain him.

Boyd watched him go. "You're keeping bad company, Mrs. James."

I said nothing.

"Some people think they can break the rules. But there's a penalty for breaking rules." His voice was soft and modulated again. "Unless, of course, you're the one making them." The corner of his mouth jutted up with sudden pride. "I'm calling the shots on this one."

The dog snarled, pricking its ears. Hearing something move in the darkness, Boyd and I both turned. A skunk ambled at the edge of the clearing. The dog jumped and spun in midair, bursting into a spasm of yelps.

"One skunk breeds another," Boyd said.

Instinctively, the skunk turned and raised its tail. Boyd tugged the dog away.

"Think about what I've said, Mrs. James," he said, then walked away, disappearing into the darkness.

I watched them go. After a while I heard a truck start, then drive off. I followed the sound until I could no longer hear it. Heart pounding, I heard the short, sharp noises of someone sawing wood, then realized it was the sound of my own breathing. I made myself take several long, steady breaths, trying to calm myself.

"Hard to believe some people actually like that man," Harley said, appearing again. In one easy sweep, he reached down and gathered up the skunk. "At least, a skunk acts like a skunk and doesn't pretend to be anything else."

Gently he brought the skunk over and placed it on my lap. "Don't worry. He can't spray. Though he tries hard enough. Some city people had him as a pet – took his sprayer out. Then they dumped him. I call him 'Streak'."

"That's a good name," I managed to whisper, feeling overwhelmed. Too much was happening too fast. Slowly I raised my hand and began to pet the skunk. I could feel the heat of Harley's hand beside mine.

"You're shaking," he said, taking my hands in his. A stream of warmth entered my fingers and flooded through my body. The leathery smell of him filled my lungs. Feeling tears, I let my head fall and rest on his shoulder.

Very slowly, he put his hand on the top of my head and drew his palm down my back , rhythmically stroking my hair, my neck, my shoulders and the length of my spine. "My grandmother used to do this when I was a kid. If I was scared."

"It feels lovely," I whispered. Reaching over, Harley undid the chain around my waist. His gesture was as intimate as if he were undoing my clothing. My insides rose towards him like a stadium of cheering fans.

Harley edged himself away and regarded me quizzically. He took the skunk from my lap and placed it in a covered basket he'd stashed behind a tree. "I'll make a fire." He began gathering twigs.

"Boyd better not come back," I said, worried about the fire.

"He'd have a long way to walk."

"What do you mean?"

Harley smiled simply as he arranged a circle of stones

for a fire pit. "I left enough gas in his pickup to get him about three blocks from home."

"You took gas out of Boyd's truck?"

"A man like that's safest at home."

I grinned and watched his large, paw-like hands stroke the skins of the twigs before feeding them to the fire. The flames flickered up, illuminating his body in a warm, golden light.

His face was wide, with a broad, generous forehead and large, very round, black-brown eyes. It was a kind, benevolent face, both old and young. Again I had the feeling of knowing him.

When he turned, I saw the scar. It was a nasty looking thing, a slash of white and gristly skin on his neck, just under his ear. It made me wince to look at it. Whose knife had done that?

Harley rolled his jacket up for me to sit on and settled himself on a stone near the fire.

"What do you do out there in the world?" he asked.

"I counsel people," I answered, sounding steadier than I felt.

"A shrink? You're a shrink?" His tone was incredulous.

"No," I protested, "I'm a psychotherapist."

"What's the difference?" His tone was challenging, wary.

"Shrinks, as you call them, work more with drugs. I focus on dreams."

Harley looked into the fire. "My mother had a shrink once. Pumped her so full of drugs she couldn't see straight. Uppers. Downers. Relaxants. Sleeping pills. He was a drug pusher worse than any I've seen." He stared into the flames without speaking. "He never thought that maybe she was

depressed for a reason. Knew nothing about Indians or
what it was like for a native woman to marry a white man.
And have nine kids. My mom would go in black and blue
from a beating and he'd hand her stupid pills."

I nodded. I knew enough to stay out of the way when
someone was gearing up to tell their story.

A mud-slide of words came towards me. Sad, sad
words that told of a mother gone crazy, a boy forced to go
with a social worker to the mental hospital in order to see
her. Then foster families. One after another. All white.
Until a brief time when his mother got better. Not well,
but better. How he learned to be careful. To help out. No
lip. No backtalk. No talk at all for two years after he found
her body swinging from the rafters.

More homes. More shrinks. All trying to make him
talk about the suicide. Or talk at all. Bring my mother
back, he screamed at them inside himself. Then I'll talk.

He stopped his story and put his finger on the bark of
a nearby tree, stroking where someone had cut initials into
the wood.

"Too many cuts and you get weakened. The bugs get
in. You die slowly. From the outside in. That's what
happened to her." Harley was quiet, but he was breathing
heavily. He closed his eyes. Slowly I felt him calm and the
words he'd spoken settled like rubble around him.

"After she died, I stole. Stole everything I could lay my
hands on. The cops threw me into reform school." He
touched the scar on his neck. "That's where I got this
thing. Then they threw me into jail. But as soon as I got
out, I stole again. So they started beating me. Finally, I got
my head straight and came back to the reserve. Learned
leather. Got sane." He paused and grinned. "Or saner."

"You have to be a little crazy to be sane these days," I offered softly. Harley grunted gratefully. "How did you know to go back to the reservation?"

Harley smiled. "Same way you knew to chain yourself to a tree. Your body just gets fed up. Starts giving its own orders."

I nodded. I wanted to go over and hold him.

As if needing to get away from the debris of his words, Harley stood up and made his way down to the water. In a few minutes, I heard a splash. I followed the sound.

Standing near the shore in the dark tree shadows, I watched the moon making a long cone of shimmering silver on the lake. Out of the glittering water swam Harley, his naked body gliding through the water as sleekly as an otter. When he was near the shore, he climbed on a large rock and sat staring at the lake, his long hair making a dark line down the muscles of his back. After a time of stillness, he spoke.

"Come swimming."

Taken aback that he knew I was watching, I stammered,

"No, I . . ."

"You want to."

I smiled. He was right. Even though I knew it would be brutally cold, I wanted to. Or, at least part of me wanted to. But there were other, more restrictive parts of myself to contend with. *What if someone saw you? Swimming with a half-breed?* The voices of my socialization never stopped, even in the middle of the night in the middle of nowhere.

In a moment's determination, I took off my clothes and the incessant inner chatter seemed to drop away with the falling fabric. I'd been denied this pleasure too often as a child and had vowed never to pass by such opportunities when I was old enough to choose for myself. Unfortunately, for years I'd kept such a tight leash on my life, the choice hadn't even been possible. Until tonight. I dove into the water.

The coldness took my breath away. The water pressed itself against my body, sliding over every part of me with erotic intimacy, entering me in my most private places. Exploding with sensations, I soared out of the water like a fish. When I could hold the lunge no more, I splashed down into the black, black water.

When I came out of the lake, my teeth were chattering. Harley held his jacket out to me. Wrapping it around me, I felt myself tip forward into his arms. His body was like a slow, strong drumbeat of heat. I waited for him to let me go, but he kept hold of me. Warm droplets of water from his skin slid into my hands.

Was he going to kiss me? He pulled his head back. With the angle of the moon, one part of his face was bathed in light, the other dark in shadow. As I looked at him, I sensed the pain and beauty of his whole life.

Our mouths found each other. His lips tasted as fresh as the lake, but warmer, sweeter.

What are you doing? Stop this at once. But my mouth was lost in his lips. The scolding voice inside my head was very far away and I could hardly hear it over the lovely feelings rising in my body.

After the kiss, Harley eased himself away and walked back to the fire.

Shivering in his jacket, I stood still. My God, what was happening to me? Who was this person standing naked in the forest kissing a man she had just met? Self-conscious and confused, I made myself get dressed and moved towards my sleeping bag. Harley, back in his clothes, came and sat beside me near the fire.

Harley rearranged some of the burning logs with his boot. "We better get this out," he said. The logs, removed from the intensity of the flames, smoked thickly. Before putting the fire out completely, Harley reached into his pocket and tossed something on the last of the flames. The strong smell of cedar filled the air. Drawing a feather from his hat, he swept the billows of white smoke around my body in a ritual he seemed to know well.

Sensing the sacredness of the act, I shut my eyes. The smoke felt strong and smelled lovely.

"A little Indian protection," Harley explained. He dispersed the embers and the blackness of the night swooped down around us. We sat in the dark without speaking for a long time. Slowly, the dim light of day crept around us.

"Scared?" Harley finally asked. I nodded. "You know what my grandfather used to say about fear?" He lifted his open hand to face me and parodied, "Fear, big horse. Learn ride, go anywhere."

I smiled. Words were beyond me now and in the gathering quiet, the situation I was about to face loomed over me. Shortly, I was going to be arrested. Arrested. Put in jail like a common criminal. I, who had never even had a speeding violation. How had all this happened? Suddenly I felt completely hopeless.

"I can't believe I'm doing this," I whispered.

Harley looked at me with calm understanding. His

face was broad and open, as though it had room for many things. It made me feel peaceful just looking into it.

"Life is more sudden than we think sometimes," he said softly. "Changes grow underground and we don't know they're there until they burst out."

"I just wish there was some other way. Something not so public. Like a petition." I was trying to convince myself of other options.

Harley scowled. "You'd keep your hands clean that way, sure. But there's nothing wrong with digging into the dirt. These trees of yours have as much of themselves in the dirt as in the sky."

"But being arrested is so humiliating."

He shrugged. "Some of the world's greatest people have spent time in the clinker. Gandhi, Martin Luther King, and who was that woman who fought for the vote, Pank—"

"Pankhurst. Emmeline Pankhurst."

"I've spent a few days in there myself. Probably will spend more too, before I'm done. Sometimes you've got to put your body where your heart is and say 'no'." Seeing the worry on my face, he added, "Trust yourself. Don't let that mind of yours analyse everything upside-down and sideways. A person's thinking can make anything right. Or anything wrong. You can't think your way through this one. The point is, you did something. Even if nothing happens, you took action. That's better than what the rest of this town is doing right now."

"Will you stay with me when the police come?"

He looked at me with tender eyes as if he knew his response was going to be hard. "I'll stay until they come. But no longer. This isn't my cause."

"What is your cause?" I asked him as disappointment sank inside me.

"We got kids sniffing gas," he answered seriously. "It doesn't feel right to take on anything else while that's going on."

I frowned, remembering something in the news recently about two Indian boys dying from inhaling gasoline fumes. The very thought of it made me feel sick.

"Is there much you can do?"

Harley shrugged. "I've taught some how to make drums. There's a few drumming circles going now. That usually brings them back to themselves. If anything will."

I sighed. I didn't understand what he meant about drumming circles, but I knew now was not the time to ask. It was getting light. I wanted to walk through the woods again. Giving Harley's shoulder a supportive squeeze, I wandered through the trees. An early morning mist was snaking itself through them so thickly I could hardly see their trunks. It was as if the mist were trying to hide the trees in its cloudy vapours. Despite the fog, I could feel the presence of the trees. They were as alive as people.

Further on, the mist was lighter and I could see The Lovers entwined rapturously in each other's limbs. Big Red stood noble and still. Candelabra, with its finger-shaped offshoots, looked like a giant hand reaching up to heaven.

In the moist morning air, the smell of the trees was strong and pungent. I looked up into a branch. Soon it would be full of hundreds of newly-fledged leaves. I loved baby leaves, they looked just like hands.

As I passed, I touched each tree with my open palm.

Their skins felt as familiar as my own children's. Beneath the bark I felt a peace and strength as deep and old as the planet itself. Had Boyd ever let his fingers run down the smooth skin of a beech tree? Or felt the aged wisdom of a pine? I liked to think he hadn't.

To Boyd, these trees were merely impediments to his monetary success. And money was important to a man like Boyd. Money was important to a lot of people. Not that I had anything against money. It was just that people were letting it become more important than other things.

I knew every society had its share of greedy people, but the numbers of people out for themselves seemed to be growing. I wouldn't have been so worried if there were dozens of other people working hard to keep the greedy people in their places. But there weren't. That's what saddened me. And frightened me too. For it gave people like Boyd power.

"The Granny Group," I said suddenly. "I've got the Granny Group today." I checked my watch. I was due there to lead an exercise class. I rushed back to Harley. "Can you wait here for fifteen minutes? I've got to do something." Harley assented without question.

I jogged the two blocks to Aggie's where the group usually met. Aggie's house was a lovely, old-fashioned mansion overlooking the lake. When I arrived, the Grannies were waiting, as I thought they would be, sitting in a colourful diversity of exercise outfits. Some had hearing aids, but many refused to wear them and were shouting their conversations to each other.

"Don't you ladies ever sleep?" I asked, moving quickly to the front of the room. These old women always made me feel good. "It's only six-forty-five."

"Four hours every night," Joey said, her thick body positioned on her mat like a sitting bull. "Whether we need it or not!" She slapped her sausage-shaped thigh and laughed. "That reminds me," she said, turning to the group. "Did I tell you about the kid that called me an 'old lady'?" She made a face of great displeasure. "I told him! Said, 'Don't you call me an old lady. I ain't no lady!'" Her large head bobbed up and down as she laughed.

I smiled, despite my agitation. I loved the humour in this group. Old people went one way or the other, serious as cadavers or funny as comedians. I started to talk, but Agatha jerked to attention, her jowls jiggling.

"Goodness gracious, Jessica! What did you do to your hair?"

I hated being called Jessica, but answered Agatha as evenly as I could. "I was swimming."

"I think it's rather nice," Grace offered, moving her small fragile fingers along the white curls that framed her petite face. "More natural."

Agatha sniffed and blinked her eyes. "I wouldn't dream of touching my own hair."

"Not everyone is rich enough to go to a hairdresser every week," Joey said.

"Not everyone cares about their appearance," Agatha retorted icily.

As usual, I thought, being with the Grannies was a world of its own. I pressed on. "Listen, I've only come to tell you I can't do the class this morning. Estelle, could you lead it this once?"

Estelle lifted her stork-like neck and nodded her patrician head demurely.

"Why can't you do it?" Grace said, her thin, small mouth petulant.

"She's chained herself to a tree of all things," Agatha decreed, as if I had been doing a striptease in the park. "So they can't cut it down." Mouths dropped open and the group broke into comments and questions.

"You mean one of the big ones in the park?" Grace asked, her voice trembling as it did whenever she became upset. "Some of those trees are as old as I am."

Estelle's marble-sized eyes bulged. "Jessie, you might get arrested," she said, her tone full of worried concern.

I nodded soberly.

"They're the ones who should be in jail, the people who want to cut them down." Joey shifted her weight on the mat ominously.

"Imagine arresting someone as well-intentioned as you," Estelle said in her proper British accent. "Someone trying to do a good deed."

"I used to play with those trees when I was little," Agatha said, her voice warm with nostalgia.

"It's like cutting us down," Grace commented bleakly.

"I've got to go." I edged towards the door. "I'll see you next week – I hope!"

Worried now that I'd been away far too long, I raced out the door and collided with someone coming in. It was Elfreda. I helped steady the old woman, then hurried on.

Back at the park, I saw that Harley had packed up my sleeping bag and made a neat pile of my things.

"I can drop this stuff over to your house later if you like," he offered.

"All right. And would you feed my dog?"

"Sure. But don't worry. They won't keep you forever.

You'll get bail. They gave me bail, but then I wasn't as bad an outlaw as you."

I laughed despite my nervousness. In a few moments it would be all over. Chaining myself back in again, I sat quietly. A wind came up and I closed my eyes so I could feel the loveliness of it.

After awhile, I heard a vehicle approach. I opened my eyes. Looking down the road, I saw a truck pull up near the park. Behind it was Tamlin in a police van.

"My carriage to the county jail," I commented wryly.

With a hacksaw in his hand, Tamlin came towards me, dismal but resolute. I fought and kicked, cussed and made as much commotion as possible. In my mind. But reason censored the fantasy and I told Harley to unchain me. "No use wrecking the chain," I said dispiritedly.

Tamlin took me by the arm and led me away. His touch was gentle.

"I wish I didn't have to do this," he said quietly.

I nodded. I understood. "Each of us has to do what we have to do." The chain saw men took their saws out and made ready. I took a last look at the trees. What a colossal thud those trees were going to make coming down. Enough to shake up the whole town, I hoped.

Reluctantly, I got into the back of the van. Tamlin put the vehicle in gear and began to drive away. We were circling the edge of the park when the van slowed. There were people on the road. Probably coming to watch the trees being felled, I thought. They won't come to stop it, but they'll come to watch and complain.

I leaned forward to look. Elfreda was out front, followed closely by Joey, her jaw set at a belligerent angle. Then Estelle and Grace. Agatha Bagshaw was bringing up the rear, looking indignant and authoritative. The Grannies brought the van to a halt!

I tried to open my door, but there was no handle. Seeing Curt bend over to start his saw, I shouted, "The trees!"

The Grannies moved as one, striding towards the men and surrounding them. Knowing he could do nothing against so large a group, Tamlin sped forward. Looking out the back window, I was just in time to see Elfreda pinching Curt's behind and the chain saw falling to the ground.

Chapter 5

There were two cells in the courthouse and I was put in the first. Along the front of the cell were bars and high up on one side was a window which faced a brick wall. The only item of furniture was a thin, black iron cot.

Feeling exhausted, I propped the thin pillow against the back of the bed and sat with my arms wrapped protectively around my bent knees. On the wall by the side of the bed someone had written FUCK THE WORLD in an angular, childlike scrawl. Someone else had crossed out THE WORLD and written YOU above it. Someone else had written YEAH, FUCK ME! beside that. Alongside were various hearts with arrows slashed through them and the names and phone numbers to call "for a good time."

The room felt strange to me, as if the anguish of the previous prisoners had been pressed into the very walls. And the smell! Despite the nose-stinging aroma of disinfectant, the smell of pee was so strong I looked to see if there were still a puddle somewhere on the floor.

Usually, I liked the contained feeling of small spaces. Everything about this room, however, felt cold, hard and punishing. Had Harley been in this jail? I tried to imagine him here and felt oddly comforted by the thought of this possibility.

Lying down, I pulled the thin grey blanket over

myself. Were the Grannies still at the park? Would they get arrested too? At any moment I might hear a gaggle of voices and see them herded into the next cell. The minutes passed. Should I be calling someone? Wasn't that what people were supposed to do when they were arrested? Make their one phone call? But who would I call?

I lay down and tried to sleep, but I couldn't. Finally, I asked if I could use the phone and called home. The other end of the phone was picked up and I was just about to speak when I heard my own cheerful voice on the answering machine. Robyn must still be asleep. She probably didn't even know I hadn't come home. She might not realize it until half the day was over. Disgruntled, I realized she probably wouldn't even bother picking up my messages, so I didn't bother leaving one.

Needing to hear a friendly voice, I overrode my intuition and tried Madge. Madge was an early riser, so I knew she'd answer. Her phone rang and rang. A thought hardened my tummy. Was she off with some man? My breath caught in my throat. Was Madge at Boyd's? Had she spent the night with him? Was that why she hadn't come back to see me, because she was off screwing Boyd?

Muttering furiously, I returned to my cell. I felt utterly defeated. Lying on the hard cot, I slept fitfully.

Later, Madge appeared at the jail to get me out, but as she stood in front of my cell, she peeled her face off like a mask. Underneath she was as highly painted as a prostitute. In the distance, I could hear someone sobbing. Then Rudi was gently telling me to wake up. When I did awake, the thin pillow was wet from my tears.

I forced myself to sit up. During my therapy with Rudi, she had often told me to wake up. "You live in la-la land," she used to tell me. "You can't just have the pretty part. Even if you could, you'd be missing out on half of what life is all about. Remember, along with the light goes the dark."

"But I don't want that part," I used to tell her. "It's too hard."

"Only because you don't know how to handle it. Wouldn't you rather learn than always be on the run from it, like your mother?"

Under her tutelage, I had slowly learned. But it wasn't easy. It still wasn't easy. To this day, I resisted seeing the dark side of people. I wanted the world to be a safe, easy place with safe, easy people. Who treated me nicely. I could almost hear Rudi's low chuckle. She was such a wise old thing. I yearned to hear her voice. She was the person I should have called. Just hearing her voice would have helped.

After a time, a bald man in a guard's uniform appeared, jangled a key and opened the door.

"You're outta here," he said.

I stared at him disbelievingly. Didn't I have to pay some sort of fine or go before a judge?

"Go," the man said. "Before someone changes their mind." He walked me to the outside door and opened it.

I hesitated. Why was I being let go? Had someone pulled strings? Part of me thought I should stay, insist on the due process of the law, but my body strode forward into the sunlight. Within minutes I was home. Charlie yipped and jumped at the sight of me. When I leaned down to pet him, I noticed a long, black feather tied to his collar. Harley had obviously been here to walk him. I smiled and made my way to the shower, Charlie following devotedly.

After I had washed the smell and feel of the jail off my body, I wandered through the house trying to settle myself. Was Robyn home? I wasn't about to call down. I wanted life to be smooth and uncomplicated for awhile, so I busied myself watering plants.

Slowly, the soothing presence of the house wrapped itself around me. I loved my house. In the living room, fig and rubber trees, ten feet high, dwarfed the furniture. Huge peat baskets, trailing long vines, hung from the ceiling. Along every window were dozens of geraniums laden with crimson balls of colour.

I hadn't intended my home to be a greenhouse, but people kept giving me plants. Plants as gifts, plants that had been abandoned, plants that were sick and needing nursing, plants that had outgrown their other homes. Tending them all took time, but I always found it soothing to take care of them. Filling a watering can, I walked from plant to plant, tipping water into the guzzling, open-mouthed pots.

When I was finished, I checked my appointment book. Thank goodness I had only booked clients for the afternoon. That would give me time to take a nap. What about the trees? Shouldn't I go down to the park and see what had happened? Maybe after I'd slept. At the moment, I couldn't face it. There was nothing I could do now anyway.

The barrage of lights on my answering machine caught my attention, but I decided I wasn't ready for messages yet either. News of what I'd done would be all over town. Were those calls from clients wanting to cancel their appointments? I shuddered at the thought and went into the sunny kitchen. Robyn's unwashed dishes filled the sink and food was scattered over the counters. Welcome home.

Robyn knew I hated a messy kitchen. In a moment of blind fury I thought about dumping the dirty dishes on her bed. I made myself breathe and slowly began to clear enough space to make myself breakfast.

Robyn had been home two weeks now and we'd hardly talked. Every time I asked her something, she acted as though I were invading her turf. As if I were the enemy. Why had she come home if she wasn't interested in spending time with me?

Too tired to figure it out, I fixed myself an egg on toast and flipped through the mail. The first thing I picked up was a brochure from a photography school. I had sent for it hoping to interest Robyn. Maybe if she enrolled in school, she'd settle down. The courses looked good and I set the pamphlet casually on top of the newspaper so Robyn might just sort of encounter it. It was best for her not to think it had come from me.

Next I perused a conference brochure. The topic of multiple personality interested me, but I didn't like the idea of spending a whole day seated in a chair. My body hated that.

"When are people going to realize we're more than heads with bodies dangling underneath?" Charlie cocked his head. "I know you've heard all this before, Charlie. You probably think I'm becoming eccentric in my old age, but eccentricity is one of the few compensations of getting old." I ate my toast. "When you get older, Charlie, you can no longer take your body for granted. It forces itself upon you – with aches and pains and needs.

"All I'm saying is that it would be nice if the world

started treating people as if we were both minds and bodies. But I guess that's too political. If people truly felt their bodies, they wouldn't be able to sit all day at conferences or smoke cigarettes or watch people being murdered on television. For that matter, if people really let themselves experience life, they wouldn't be able to cut down trees either.

"You'll be glad to know that eccentrics live longer," I said, slipping Charlie a crust of toast.

A postcard caught my eye. At the bottom of the pile of mail, it had a picture on the front of a woman with all her body parts rearranged. How strange, I thought, turning it over.

It was postmarked from France and addressed to Robyn. I was in the process of setting it aside when my eye saw the word "bitch." Before I could stop myself I began reading:

> *Dear Robbins,*
> *Yeah, parents are a drag. Your mother sure sounds like a bitch. Control freak or what! Why don'cha come back over? I think that's a great idea about Greece. Remember those Aussies we met there last time? We could hang out on Crete and get fucked every night . . .*

I dropped the card. Somehow I managed to move myself over to the couch with my tea. Charlie followed and I broke my rule and I let him up beside me. My chest felt squishy like the earth gets when it's been tramped on by too many people.

When had I been a bitch? Was it being a bitch to ask someone to clean up her dishes? Or put the garbage out? And I had thought I'd been going easy on her. Well, there was no point in carrying on with that.

It was funny the way you thought you could know someone. After Bart died and I had to sort through his possessions, I found things that surprised me. Part of a coin collection, for example. I hadn't known he was interested in coins. And there had been a business card with the name of a psychotherapist on it. Beneath the name was written "2:30 Tuesday". Had Bart been seeing a counsellor? For what?

The existence of this card stunned me. For months I kept it on my desk. I hoped that as time passed, I would forget about it. But I couldn't forget about it. One day, I got up the nerve to call. Rudi answered.

I never did find out much about Bart's time with Rudi. He'd only managed two appointments before his heart attack. And after one session with Rudi myself, I was too engrossed in my own psychological process to think about Bart's.

Yet the realization that people were often quite different from how we imagined them stayed with me, lurking at the edge of my awareness, waiting for an opportunity to pounce on someone I knew. It had certainly taken a few bites out of my image of Madge. And now, this morning, it had devoured Robyn.

Get fucked every night? Was this Robyn's idea of a good time? And Greece. I hadn't even known she'd been to Greece. That hurt. That I knew so little about her and her life. In fact, as I lay there, I wondered whether the Robyn I saw was a complete figment of my imagination.

Sometimes, when I got really stuck in a personal problem, I tried to think what I'd do if the same situation had come to me via a client. So, at a loss about what else to do, I created Jane Smith, who arrived in my office and told me about reading a postcard of her daughter's, just like the one I had just read.

I knew immediately what Jane Smith needed to do. She had to be helped to examine her attachment to the image she had of her daughter. She had to be helped to let go and see her daughter more realistically.

Am I attached to an image of Robyn that isn't realistic?

You most certainly are. And you're attached to what happens between you. You want to have long chats over lunch with her. To go shopping together. You want to be buddies. But that's not the kind of person Robyn is.

Who is she then?

Find out.

Yes. But that would mean letting go of my dream for her.

Charlie nuzzled my hand. "Why can't my children be more like you, eh, Charlie? Devoted, easy to get along with. Always ready with a wag of the tail."

I scratched his neck, just under his collar where I knew he liked it best. "And to think, I almost took you to the pound."

The day of Charlie's arrival was long past now, but the intensity of that day made the memory vivid. Bart had died a few months earlier and Robyn had already disappeared to Europe the previous year. Ted was working in Ottawa.

One grey November morning I was still in bed when someone knocked at the door.

"Bloody Hell," I hissed, dragging the covers with me

as I peeked out the bedroom window. There, in a duck yellow rain slicker was Madge, holding something in her arms. Madge was kicking at the door with her boot. Determined to ignore the world, I tried to go back to sleep, but the incessant banging continued.

"About time," Madge growled when I finally gave up and went to the door.

"You could have used the bell."

"Not with this in my arms." She thrust the bundle forward. Something warm and wiggly landed in my arms.

Madge pushed forward into the vestibule. "It's a puppy," she stated flatly.

"I don't want a puppy."

"I didn't say you did." Madge took a deep breath. "I'm the one who wants you to have a dog. It's like death city in this house. You don't have to die just because Bart did."

I shook my head, spitting with anger. Everyone had their ideas and opinions. But no one, no one understood. It wasn't grief that was getting me. It was the emptiness. The vast, empty uselessness of my life. With nothing to distract, no one to take care of, my sense of myself stretched like a wasteland around me. I had no idea who I was or what I wanted. I couldn't decide what to have for breakfast, what to wear, what to do. Day after day I stayed in bed.

"I brought you the dog because I had to do something," Madge said, her voice turning softly confessional. "What you do with him is up to you."

"I'll take him to the pound," I threatened.

"If you want to be that stupid, go ahead." Tossing her head back, she left, slamming the door behind her.

The puppy, frightened by the noise, poked its head up

through the blanket, looked mournfully at me and attempted to lick my hand.

"You looked as miserable as I felt," I explained to Charlie as he cuddled beside me. "I guess that's why I kept you." Massaging his ear, I added, "Thank goodness things got better, eh? Rudi. School. Buying this house." I sighed. "It's been a long haul."

Leaning back, I realized how exhausted I was. How was I supposed to carry on when I felt like this? A little whiskey in my tea would help. Just this once. Just this morning. I put my hand over the top of my cup as if to censor myself. I didn't ever want to rely on liquor as a support. That was too like my mother.

Drinking problems hopscotched their way through every generation of my family. My great-grandfather had owned a whiskey mill in Scotland and sipped its vintage from morning until night. His son, my grandfather, had become a teetotaller in reaction. My father thought abstinence was ridiculous, yet, remarkably, managed to control his own drinking well. Unfortunately, he could not control his wife's. My mother, he soon found out, only found life bearable if she were soaked in an anaesthetic amount of gin.

My earliest memories were of my mother staying in bed. Of course, nothing was ever said about why my mother wasn't well, or why, yet again, family plans had to be cancelled. I was praised for being the "little mom" and grew up to become my father's confidante and social companion.

"It wasn't until I worked with Rudi that I recognized how cheated I felt," I told Charlie. "How ripped off! I needed a childhood. And since I couldn't have my own, I had to create one for someone else. Which, of course, is where Robyn came in. Poor thing. She was born right into the part."

I had yearned for a little girl. I had been happy about Ted as my first born, but I desperately wanted a girl. When Robyn arrived, I was over the moon. Young Ted was moved to his own room and the nursery transformed into a fairyland with thick folds of white silk skirting the antique wicker bassinet, appliquéd stars and moons shining from the ceiling and stuffed animals everywhere. A music box tinkled magical tunes for hours at a time.

I made sure everything in Robyn's world was soft and safe. No stories of witches and trolls for my little girl. Peter Rabbit's adventures with Mr. McGregor were as tough as things got. Immersed in animal stories, walks in the woods and the rich make-believe world of stuffed animals, Robyn grew into a true nature child. Birds took bread from her palms, squirrels ran up her arms and once, in the spring, I found Robyn standing with dozens of wasps wandering around her extended arms.

When Robyn reached puberty, I explained about sex, about how a man and woman became close physically when they loved each other.

"Is that the only time it happens?" Robyn had asked, wide-eyed and trusting.

"Yes," I had replied, ignoring an uncomfortable twinge in my stomach. There was time enough to introduce Robyn to the seamier side of life. I liked children to be children and was pleased that Robyn showed an ingenuous naiveté so rare in modern children.

"Oh, Charlie, you see what a set-up Robyn was born into? Do you see why it led to such a mess? I was trying to give her the childhood I never had. I never wanted her to grow up." I sighed heavily. In the bleariness of my tiredness, my whole life felt like a failure.

As if to rescue me from the painful thoughts, a wash of sleepiness drifted over me. In the background I heard the phone ringing and ringing, but leaving the machine to answer, I let myself be pulled down into the relieving undertow of sleep.

Chapter 6

My body is hard, folded into itself like a small bud. Deep inside, at my very centre, a pressure builds, threatening to push me into a new, unfathomable shape. The casing of my body tears and I am frightened. Desperately I try to hold back the forces. I am not ready. I am not ready. But the contractions begin, pushing me, thrusting me forward, wrenching me out of the shape I know myself to have. Shouting with terror, I start to come apart. To my amazement, I do not break, but burst out into a blossom.

I awoke smiling. As the dream slipped away, I became aware of Charlie yawning beside me. Stretching, I checked the time. My God, I had to get going. A client was due in just a few minutes.

Damn. There was no time to find out about the trees now. All for the best, I thought. As valiant as the Grannies' attempts might be, I doubted that a group of seniors could stop the inevitable. And I didn't think I could face seeing the huge bodies of the trees on the ground.

Quickly, I got ready for an afternoon of clients. Speeding past my answering machine, I noticed the flashing light, but I didn't have time to attend to the messages the machine told me were waiting. Would Harley be one of them?

I ran a comb through my hair, went to my office and lit a candle. Lighting a candle was a Rudi ritual, something I always did to remind myself of the sacred space so necessary for inner exploration. It was also an act of homage. Lighting the candle always brought the feeling of Rudi back. I remembered the hours I'd spent pouring my heart out to Rudi while a candle offered its redeeming light.

The doorbell rang. I took a deep breath and began my afternoon. Sarah was first. Sarah had been five when her father shot himself. Now, twenty years later, she talked about her fear of trusting a man who had recently showed interest. We spent most of the session exploring ways she might allow herself to get to know the man better and feel safe at the same time.

Leslie was next. Leslie was a young artist who wanted to explore her dream world. In her session, she dared to confront a frightening dream figure who, by the end of her work, turned into a friend. The session was an exciting one for both of us and she hugged me warmly at the end.

Donna was the third client. Lately in her therapy, memories of childhood sexual abuse had emerged. Because the abuse had started when she was very small and the inappropriate touching had been intertwined with the normal touching of day to day life, it had been difficult to recognize.

"Now I know why I'm nervous in the bathtub," Donna said, chewing on a long strand of hair in the same way that Robyn sometimes did. "I only figured it out when Doug stayed that weekend because he came into the bathroom and asked if he could wash my back. It freaked me right out. That's when I remembered."

Donna had been dating Doug for two months now, but it was hard for her to commit herself to just going out with one man. My guess was that as long as she continually distracted herself with men, she wouldn't have to face the unresolved issues of her past. For often when someone tried to step forward in their lives, they were forced to feel the ball and chain of unfinished business.

"My father gave me a bath every night," Donna said. "Told me how important it was that we wash the 'secret places.' Then he made me wash his 'secret places.' The bastard. But you know what the really crazy part was? I didn't even know what he was doing was wrong. That's the part that really hurts. That my mother . . ." her voice cracked. "There I was being fondled, abused, each and every day and my mother didn't even help me to know what was going on. I mean, I thought licking your father's penis was what every daughter did. It used to really confuse me when my girlfriends used to giggle about catching a glimpse of their dad's dick. I saw my father's dick every damned day."

Angrily, she wiped at her eyes with her sleeve. "My mother always talked about how helpful my father was – so willing to dress us and bath us. And feel us up." Her voice became loud and demanding. "How could she not have known? What did she think he was doing with the bedroom door closed, reading me bedtime stories?"

I nodded sympathetically. The abuse had been destructive enough to Donna, but her mother's complicity made the damage all the worse. It was amazing what people didn't see. But back then, when Donna was a child, people hadn't the foggiest idea that sexual abuse occurred in families. Even when the signs were all around, people often failed to see them. If you don't know a certain animal exists, you're hardly going to recognize its footprints. I felt slightly sick to my stomach. I hoped I wasn't getting the flu.

"When I was ten, my friend Judy saw a man exposing himself and she told her mother. Her mother had an absolute fit. She called the police, even went out in search of the guy. That's when I started to realize. That's when I began to know that what my father was doing to me wasn't right. But I kept thinking, if it's not right, why doesn't my mother stop it?

"That's what infuriates me now. That my mother didn't help me." She took a big breath and pushed out the final words, "She didn't protect me."

I laid my hand on my stomach. It was cramping badly now. This definitely felt like the flu.

"So I called her. Told her the whole shit load."

Donna's words brought me back to the moment. "You told her about your father?"

"I figured now that my father was dead, she'd hear me." Her eyes became pleading. "You know what she said? She said, 'Don't be silly, Donna, your father would never have done anything like that.'" Covering her face with her hands, she moaned, "Why didn't she believe me? Why didn't she realize?" Donna cried for the rest of her session, as fragile as a child. I felt sicker than ever.

My last appointment of the afternoon was with Norman. Wearily, I led him down to my office. Noticing his pale face and dry lips, I offered him some water. I sipped a glass myself, hoping this might calm my stomach.

I sat quietly, waiting for him to begin. I liked to give people a few moments to adjust to the therapeutic space.

For many people, being authentic and feeling-based was the antithesis of how they functioned in the rest of their lives, and it often took a few moments to settle in.

As I waited, I focussed my attention on Norman. A sandy-haired man with boyish freckles and an athletic frame, he wore a tee-shirt that read: "The One With The Most Toys Wins".

A highly paid executive, Norman had all the accoutrements of success: memberships in clubs, political connections, money. Yet, despite the businesslike persona he presented, I sensed a tender, gentle spirit struggling to emerge. Not that Norman would ever admit this. I doubted whether he even knew this part of him existed. What he did know, and what had brought him to therapy a few months ago, was that from the moment when he woke up in the morning, depression pressed down on him like a lid.

Norman began the session by doing a lengthy review of what was happening at work, going on at length about a particular co-worker who refused to listen to anyone. This was what I found challenging about working with Norman, his inability to get down to the bones of himself.

As I listened, I felt uneasy. I watched his eyes flash about the room restlessly. Then, unable to hold back, his eyes pounced on me.

Something's wrong. Something's wrong, they said, then hurled themselves up the wall behind me to the bookshelf.

A classic double message, I thought, wondering if I dared bring the incongruity to his attention. I thought not. If I attempted to make the secondary message conscious, Norman would probably just deny it and the message might get even further repressed. Besides, I didn't feel up to confrontation today.

As I listened to him talk and observed his body language, as I always did, I noticed his head was moving slightly from side to side as if it were refuting what his mouth was saying.

It always fascinated me how a person could be saying one thing in words while their body said something completely different in gestures. Bodies had a way of getting their messages in, however sneakily they had to do it. That was why I always paid attention to both the verbal and the nonverbal cues. The latter were a major source of information.

All bodies talked: they squirmed, yawned, trembled, went hard, went soft, sighed, coughed and made a hundred other gestures that told their own story, usually to the complete oblivion of the person talking. Even those clients who had learned the art of suppressing this "talk", usually found that, despite their attempts at control, these insurgent impulses simply went underground. There, like guerrilla forces in the jungle, they could cause all kinds of trouble, showing up as ailments or symptoms and sometimes, even serious illnesses.

Bodies amazed me. They could do the most incredible things. From one client to another, the mood of my office could change as dramatically as if someone had thrown a can of paint against the wall. It could be black paint or red or even bright yellow, but each and every client had a way of painting the room their own inimitable colour. Textures and temperatures changed too. During some sessions, I could feel grief literally dripping from the furniture or fury heating up the carpet.

Norman was talking about his childhood now, telling me about the lodge his parents owned and how he always had to work.

"I never got to do what I wanted," he lamented. "When my father died, I had to take over as manager. I remember because I had planned a ski trip and couldn't go. The trip was to Switzerland. I'd always wanted to go to Switzerland. Anyway, I had to cancel the trip. I told myself I'd go the next year, but I never did. The needs of the lodge took over. My mother kept telling me what a fortune we'd make on the place if we built it up and she was right. We ended up selling the business for a fortune. But that was many years of hard work later."

"What about the part of you that wanted the ski trip? What happened to that part?"

"Reality," he answered flatly. "Some things just aren't possible."

I frowned. People were so willing to limit themselves. Yes, limitations were a fact of life, but many were self-imposed.

"You don't make money out of being a skier," Norman concluded crisply, like putting a lid on a tin box.

"Is making money the most important thing?" I challenged. I felt like I was listening to his mother talking. "What about the part of you that wants to ski?"

"As I said, you don't make money skiing."

I sighed. Where did Norman get the idea that his life was a lump of clay to be manipulated into whatever shape he desired? I'd seen it so many times, people dressing themselves up in a certain "personality", then attempting to live it out. But it always cost them. The price tag was always a loss of vitality and energy.

If I'd learned anything as a psychotherapist, it was this: that each of us has a certain inherent nature that needs to be honoured. When it is honoured and a person lives near the truth of themselves, they are fed by the force that truth gathers. When they live distant from that source, they are bereft of their innermost juices. As if their souls were starved, these people have to make do with ersatz supplies of nourishment, like power or prestige, which have to be continually replenished.

Norman struck me as one of those people who had been dressed up at a very early age to be someone he wasn't. It seemed to me only a matter of time until the truth about himself would demand recognition.

Noting my own finger tapping, I realized I wanted to move past this commentary Norman was engrossed in. Otherwise, I'd start thinking about the trees again. So, the next time his eyes came my way, I said into them voicelessly, "I'm listening. You can tell me whatever you need to say."

Norman's eyes widened. The two-track session continued with Norman and I talking while a second conversation went on with our eyes. Finally, he took a deep breath.

"Suddenly I feel depressed. Like something's about to get me," he said, swallowing hard. His eyes reached for mine.

"Can you say more?"

He shook his head resolutely. "I don't have time."

I sighed. People were always blaming time. When someone said they didn't have time, I always wanted to rephrase their words and say, "You mean you don't choose to have time." Usually people have more choices than they're willing to admit to.

"You have fifteen minutes. Time enough."

Norman pulled himself out of the chair. "I'd better get going."

"All right." I wasn't going to push him. If his psychological resources needed more time, he could have it.

Out in the hall, he pulled on an expensive jacket and moved towards the door. Turning, he tossed a goodbye over his shoulder, but his eyes caught mine and for a moment, a stillness filled the air between us.

"I'm dying," his eyes said.

My own eyes stung as I accepted the unspoken words. Norman, unconscious of the message his body had just delivered, went out the door.

For a long moment, I was unable to move. It was Charlie's head against my leg that made me realize I was staring into space, trembling. Then, as always when I was confused and needing time, I tended my plants.

Picking some dead leaves off a begonia, I shivered. Were his eyes telling me about a symbolic death or a real one? I knew he'd had cancer once. Years ago. Said he'd "got rid of it" by having a section of his bowel removed.

Was it really possible to get rid of something like that? Was a disease a mere anatomical anomaly that could be removed by the flick of a surgeon's knife? It reminded me of the way unhappy spouses got "rid" of their partners, as if the partners were the problem. I shook my head. Why couldn't people take more responsibility for what they were creating in their lives?

For example, is it a coincidence when a person gets one abusive partner after another? Or repeatedly gets sick? I don't think so. What shows up in our lives repeatedly is not simply a case of bad luck, however hard we want to believe it is.

The partners people choose and the diseases people develop, are usually not simply events that happen "out there", but situations they are part of creating. Not creating consciously, but deep in their unconscious, as part of their life plan. Until people accept that and are willing to see their part in each and every aspect of their creations, they'll continue to be plagued by whatever it is they are plaguing themselves with. In my experience, the only way out, is through.

What if Norman really were sick? What was his responsibility in that? Not that he would ever have chosen consciously to have cancer. But perhaps on a deeper lever, a soul level almost, there was some purpose to it. Some life lesson.

Gibberish, my mind said. But as I tended my plants, I couldn't dislodge the feeling in my belly that Norman's cancer had returned and that he was trying to warn me, prepare me before facing it himself. Oh, God, I hoped this wasn't so. I didn't want him to die. I didn't want it for his sake but also, I had to admit, I didn't want it for my sake either. I didn't want to go through it. As his therapist, I would be required to be there for him. He would need someone to go through the intense feelings, the gruesome ordeal of chemotherapy or radiation. For a therapist who had worked through their own death issues, this wouldn't be a problem. But I hadn't. When it came to death, I was still a little kid facing a monster in the dark.

Should I pass him along to another therapist! No, I couldn't run out on him like that. But how could I help him when I had my own unresolved issues about death? I hadn't even phoned the doctor back about my own tests yet.

I went to the phone to look up the doctor's telephone number. What if all these death images with Norman were projections of my own fears? What if I were the one who was ill? Even though I didn't know what was wrong with my test results, I knew they weren't right. And ever since my appointment with Donna, I'd been feeling awful. With unsteady fingers, I dialled the doctor's office.

Yes, it was true, the nurse admitted, my Pap smear had come back a little off. Probably just a mistake at the lab, but would I come in and let them try again?

So smooth that voice, I thought, so practised at easing fears back into cupboards. I made an appointment and hung up. Knowing what to do, my fingers dialled Rudi's number. Like someone who had ignored her hunger for too long and was now famished, I felt weak with need for her. As the phone rang, I felt the pressure build in me. Soon I'd be hearing Rudi's voice and all would be well. Rudi's daughter answered.

"Rudi can't come to the phone," Margaret told me. "She's sick."

"Sick?" I repeated, alarmed.

"Just a bad cold. With a touch of laryngitis, I think."

"Have you called the doctor?"

I could hear Margaret sigh. "The doctor's been. Says she'll be fine if she stays quiet."

I managed to say something about calling again tomorrow and rang off, feeling vulnerable and afraid.

No longer thinking about the trees, I went down to the lake and slipped my moss-green canoe into the water. I paddled near the shore where the surface was satin-smooth. Each time I lifted the paddle, a long chain of silver droplets cascaded down the spatula-shaped wood and dimpled the surface of the lake with ever-widening circles.

I paddled to a secluded place in the bay, then sat on the bottom of the canoe and leaned back against the seat. The boat rocked gently as the waves lapped softly against its sides. The air was moist and carried the smells of rocks and old pine needles. In a whiff, I smelled a fish. It was as if I were moving through the same air a trout had jumped into a few moments earlier. I smiled. It always struck me as magical the way fish jumped into the air, leaping so ardently into the unknown.

That made me think about death again. I'd only had two significant deaths in my life, my father's and my husband's. My father's death had been the worst. Resistant to the end, he had fought it bitterly. Whenever I'd gone to visit him in the hospital, his fear had been palpable, wrestling everyone into submission. It had been a grim-reaper kind of dying which made me anxious to think about, even now.

There were so many assumptions in a death like my father's: that death was the enemy, that death had to be fought to the bitter end and that everyone had to suffer. It presumed life was a struggle. Of course, my father's entire life had been a struggle, so his death had been strangely fitting.

In contrast to the long, drawn-out process of my father's dying, Bart's death had happened as quickly as the snap of my fingers. Friends had found him slumped in his car in the golf course parking lot, dead from a heart attack. My son had gone to identify the body. I couldn't do it myself. After watching the agonizing disintegration of my father, I didn't think I could face seeing Bart's body. Later, I'd wished I had. Not seeing the blatant reality of his death made it harder to believe. I used to catch myself looking towards the door as if expecting him to walk in at any moment.

Even though Bart's death had not been nauseating like my father's, its suddenness frightened me. For weeks afterwards, I felt nervous and oddly alert. It was difficult to trust life again. Rudi had helped me through that hard time and I needed her to help me again. But now she couldn't help. At least, not today. This was the first time Rudi had not been available to me. The thought that this could happen made my knees wobble.

She's only got a cold. Relax.

But she's eighty-one. She can't live forever.

Lots of people live into their nineties. Rudi's healthy. She has a strong constitution.

My concern over the state of Rudi's health had been the topic of many sessions. I recalled one of them vividly.

"Unfortunately," Rudi had said, "the only way you're going to know you can live without me is when you do." She'd smiled at me tenderly. "And the only way you're going to realize that death isn't frightening is when you see someone going through it unafraid."

Don't die, Rudi. Please don't die.

Not only did I abhor the idea of Rudi dying, I didn't even want death to exist. Morosely, I sat and watched the sunset. As the sun descended in the sky, it seemed to get rounder and bigger, changing from yellow to a fiery, molten red. Beneath it, the lake began to burn with silver glints, flashing and blazing with its own inner fire. The sun, dazzled by the thousands of diamonds on the water, edged towards the lake. The closer it dropped to the water, the more the lake erupted with gold and silver sparks. Right at the horizon, the water seemed to reach up towards the sun as lips swell towards a loved one. Then the sun slipped down to kiss the glittering surface while the lake reached its lip edge up and sucked the sun into its belly.

The daily death of the sun. Executed each and every night as a natural part of life. Why should my own death or someone else's death feel any different? But it did. Working through my fear of death was the last chunk of therapeutic work I had to do. But I didn't want to do it.

One thing was certain. I refused to die like my father, fighting it every step of the way. Strangely enough, I didn't want to die like Bart either. He'd missed the whole thing. What I wanted, and doubted whether I would be able to have it, was to die in the same way the sun just had, falling easily into the waters of death like a fulfilled lover, totally sated from a life fully lived. How much easier it would be to die if my life would climax in some way, surge to some satisfying crescendo, bursting with glorious colour like the sun a few moments ago.

"That's what I want," I whispered to the first star. "That's what I want."

Chapter 7

As I paddled down the lake, I heard voices. And laughter. Closer to my property, I saw a troop of people in my backyard. The entire Granny Group was waiting for me.

"We were just about to send out a search party," Elfreda shouted, striding towards me.

I looked at the woman with interest. Her cheeks were pink and her eyes glistened. "The last time I saw you, you were pinching someone's bum," I said, turning the canoe over. I stood beside her and waited, unable to ask the question that was burning in my throat.

Sensing my unspoken need, she whispered, "We saved them – at least for the moment."

My hand leapt to my chest. "Thank God."

"Don't thank God. Thank us!" She pulled off her baseball cap and threw it in the air. Charlie barked and jumped up.

I wanted to run to the phone and call Harley. Then I realized I didn't know his phone number or even where he lived.

"Aren't you going to invite us in?" demanded Joey, her hands on her bulbous hips. "You've kept us waiting long enough."

I waved them towards the house. This was cause for a celebration.

"They're a party looking for a place," Elfreda warned, elbowing my side as we joined the others. Charlie trotted happily beside her.

Within a half hour, my living room was strewn with cushions, cold drinks and pizza boxes.

Holding a piece of pizza with the very tips of her jewelled fingers, Agatha checked her watch. "Perhaps there'll be some coverage on the news."

Joey heaved forward to turn on the set.

"There we are!" Grace shrieked, her small hands flying to her delicate mouth.

Estelle reached a long, bony arm forward to turn up the volume. Parading across the screen, placards zealously jostling in front of the courthouse, were the old ladies.

I smiled, but my eyes stung at the sight of these women coming to my defence and the defence of the trees. My chest felt thick.

"That's us, all right," Joey exclaimed, turning to me. "Once we'd kicked those lumberjacks out of the park, we headed down to bust you out of jail."

"We were going to get you out of that jail if we had to break in there and pull you out ourselves," Elfreda said, her face exploding into a wild arrangement of delighted twitchings. "But that old geezer of an officer – "

"He's younger than you are." Agatha pointed at Elfreda with a manicured finger.

"Doesn't act it," Elfreda said, petting Charlie, who had his head on her lap. "Anyway, the only way he was going to release you was if we quit demonstrating. So we did."

I felt a warm softness spread over my chest. "I knew nothing of this," I said.

"My hair!" Agatha gasped, seeing herself on television. She puffed out her abundant chest indignantly.

"Sshh!" the others hissed and turned their attention back to the news.

"A public protest began today," reported the newsman, "that led to the arrest of one activist, as several of the group calling themselves 'The Guerrilla Grannies' tried to save some of the town's oldest trees."

"Guerrilla Grannies? Who gave us that name? It's preposterous!" Agatha cried.

"I like it," Joey said.

"As long as people don't think we're apes." Estelle pulled her head up like an egret and held it high above her thin, bony shoulders.

"Their leader, Mrs. Jessie James . . ."

"Jessie James! Ha!" Joey shouted. "They make you sound like an outlaw."

The reporter continued, ". . . was incarcerated today but released without charges."

The old ladies cheered. Back on television, the camera zoomed in on Elfreda. I winced. She looked as rumpled as a bag lady.

"Goodness, Freda," Agatha said, never one to let anything pass without comment, "you look like you slept in those clothes."

Elfreda stared straight ahead.

The mayor's face appeared on the television screen. Choosing his words carefully, he explained that, although the trees were a historical part of the town, they were not on town property and therefore were not in his area of jurisdiction. Furrowing his brow, he said he would look into the matter further. Meanwhile, he was asking both sides to remain calm and not to do anything rash.

"Ass covering to the last," Elfreda mused.

"There's pretty boy himself." Joey pointed a stubby finger at the television.

A glossy photograph of Boyd, looking confident, appeared on the screen.

"The owner of the property," concluded the newsman, "Mr. Boyd Murdon, a commercial developer, was unavailable for comment."

"Probably out sharpening his chain saw," Joey said, chomping her gum.

"Creep!" Elfreda shouted at the television. Beside her Charlie growled. "That's right, Charlie. Smart dog."

Grace pressed her open palms together in thanks. "But the trees! We saved the trees."

"For the moment anyway," qualified Estelle, a small smile of pleasure curving her elegant lips.

"Murdon and the mayor are probably meeting right now to see how to head off this thing," Joey speculated.

"The mayor sure looked shocked this morning," Elfreda said. "Guess he's not used to little old ladies jumping on his desk."

"You went to his office?" I asked.

"Sure did." Joey smiled at my amazement.

"While you were lolling about in jail," added Elfreda, "we all piled into Agatha's gas guzzling Caddy and hightailed it down to the mayor's. I figure if we can get him to call a community meeting about the trees, we might have a chance."

"Will he?"

"He's thinking about it. Or so he says."

"Last election Agatha was a big contributor to his campaign," Joey explained.

"Old money bags here can really throw some weight around." Elfreda smiled impishly at Agatha.

Agatha straightened her shoulders. "Just because I was a significant contributor doesn't mean he'll listen to me."

"He'll listen to you," Grace said. "Everyone listens to you."

Estelle waved her hand. "The phone!" She picked it up and spoke for a moment, then put her thin hand over the receiver. "It's the Orillia Packet and Times," she announced over the jabbering. "He wants to do a story!" She held out the phone to me.

Putting down my pineapple and olive pizza, I took the call while everyone listened. I was apprehensive at first, but the reporter's enthusiasm made it easy to talk.

"He wants to know if he can come over with a photographer," I said, putting my hand over the receiver. "Do a story on the entire group." Agatha shook her head and looked aghast, but the others nodded their heads with wide-eyed seriousness.

"Sure," I said into the phone and gave directions.

"It sounds like he was more interested in the Guerrilla Grannies than the trees." Agatha's face darkened. "I hate that name."

"That's what's going to bring them in," Joey said, nodding her head of thick white hair.

"I don't wish to be called a guerrilla," Agatha said.

Concern pulled down the creases of Elfreda's face like heavy clothes on laundry lines. "Listen, everybody, we're not going to win this because of the trees. People cut down trees all the time."

"It's perfectly legal," Joey said.

"The only way we're going to save them," Elfreda continued, "is through public opinion. And that means publicity. You don't get publicity from writing letters or being nice. You get it by being different. And old ladies fighting for things is different. Old ladies are supposed to be sweet – sweet little dried-up lavender bags. Not ass-pinching, placard-carrying activists. But that's what's going to get us the attention we need."

Joey raised her fleshy arms in the air and clapped boisterously.

Feeling an excitement whoop through my body, I added, "Elfreda's right. The only way we're going to win is to bring as much attention to our cause as we can."

"We've got to really stir things up," Joey agreed, rubbing her hands together.

"And when you think of it," I added, "seniors are the perfect group to do stuff like this. You've got the time. And you know how things work."

"And most important of all," pronounced Joey emphatically, "we know a pile of bullshit when we see it."

Everyone laughed. "On top of all that, we've got nothing to lose!" Elfreda said.

Agatha pounced. "I have a reputation to lose, thank you very much."

"Reputation? You mean as Mrs. Bagshaw? Wife of the deceased Howard Bagshaw? That's not your reputation. That's his reputation! What about getting a reputation of your own?"

Seeing the agitated look on Agatha's face, I spoke quickly. I knew just what tack to take. "Agatha, imagine your great-grandchildren reading in Who's Who: 'Agatha

Bagshaw, famous woman activist. Saved trees from being ruthlessly destroyed before the Tree Protection Act was legislated.' Wouldn't you rather have that than just being another person who never stood up for anything?"

Agatha's eyes glazed over as if she were imagining the glowing things they would write about her. The group became silent too, as if each woman were imagining her own version of historical fame.

"We could go down in history." Joey chewed her gum with renewed enthusiasm.

"Leave the world a better place," whispered Grace.

"It would make passing on so much easier." Estelle smiled wistfully.

A thoughtful quietness descended on the room. Finally Agatha spoke. "Did everyone hear that Olive passed along?"

Joey clenched her jaw. "Seventy-two and six feet under."

"Mrs. Partridge's sister went too," Estelle said, her voice barely audible.

"How old was she?'" Agatha asked.

"Too young. Far too young," Grace said.

"Sarah Beacon just found out she has cancer," Estelle added in a funereal voice.

"Age?"

"Our age," Elfreda said, looking at Agatha soberly.

Silently, I watched the women around me, deeply touched by the immensity of the hardships they faced every day. Friends and loved ones dying. Relatives getting sick. And the spectre of their own death looming. I couldn't imagine anything more difficult than being old. I knew from my work that depression and suicide were more prevalent in old age than at any other time.

"It could be any of us next," Estelle said, her eyes intense.

"I don't even buy bananas that aren't ripe." Joey smiled ruefully.

A glum despondency settled over everyone. No one spoke. The door creaked open and Robyn, dressed in black, came into the house. She was about to slip down to her quarters in the basement when Agatha noticed her.

"Robyn? Sweetheart! You're home. I heard you were, and I've been meaning to call."

"Aunt Agatha!" Robyn said, clearly surprised to find her aunt in this group. Agatha wasn't officially Robyn's aunt, but being a distant relative of Robyn's father, she had always been called that. "What are you doing here?"

"I'm wondering the same thing myself. But come, give me a kiss." She held her cheek towards Robyn. "You know, I think of you every time I look at that magnificent photograph you took of Howard, bless his soul." She tapped the seat of the chesterfield and whispered, "Come, sit beside me. We'll catch up in a little bit."

Robyn tossed her long hair back and sat down. Protectively, she folded her arms across her chest and avoided my eyes. Her face became sullen as I introduced her to those she didn't know.

While the others went on to discuss the imminent arrival of the newsman, I was quiet. In Robyn's presence I could feel my fervour shrinking. During the entire time Robyn had been home, I'd been toning myself down. Afraid of making things worse between us, I'd been careful not to show her too much of myself. But yesterday she'd caught me tied to a tree.

Life was puncturing holes in the mask of my persona and the truth of me was leaking out. These old women in their accepting, courageous way were encouraging the emergence of this new self. The trees were demanding it.

I had to make a choice. Was I going to keep trying to hide the parts of me that were frightening to Robyn or was I going to be myself, however outrageous she considered that to be? Obviously, she'd been shocked and angered by the mother she'd met yesterday. It's never easy to find out that someone close to you is not the person you thought they were. I'd just had that lesson driven home to me by Robyn's postcard.

No, if I sidestepped the ferocity of my new self, however uncomfortable that was, I would be betraying Robyn's growth process as well as my own. I'd spent too many years being untrue to myself to regress in that direction now. I was going to have to show her who I was, like it or not. Maybe that would give her the courage to show me who she was.

I smiled, remembering Robyn's look of disapproval yesterday. Usually it was the parents who disapproved of the child's radical behaviour, not the other way around. Times were certainly changing.

"What's the best thing about old age?" Elfreda suddenly called out, making a valiant attempt for levity. All eyes jumped towards her. "It beats the alternative!"

There was a burst of sudden laughter, then Joey spoke.

"So, we're all agreed – we're going to raise as much shit as we can."

Elfreda grinned. "That about sums it up. Count me in. There's no point trying to be a goody-two-shoes at this stage of my life."

"Goody-two-shoes?" Agatha cried. "That'll be the day."

"Come on, Aggie," Elfreda coached, "get that jewelled hand in the air.

"I'm in," Estelle said, nodding her head with grave nobility.

Grace and Agatha assented and everyone looked at me.

"You're in, right, Jessie?" Elfreda looked at me as if she knew something was going on but couldn't figure out what.

A swell of energy went through my body, like sap surging up the trunk of a tree in spring. "Yes!" I said and everyone but Robyn cheered.

As the meeting went on, Robyn pulled into herself. The more she withdrew, the guiltier I felt. If only I'd found myself earlier, been able to model more guts, Robyn might be a different person. Maybe she would have been able to fight back that terrible night. But how could I have taught Robyn what I hadn't known myself? I might be doing it late, but at least I was learning to stand on my own two feet now. Some women never did.

I thought about Madge. Madge would have enjoyed this free-for-all. A cold resentment prickled through me. But then I thought about Harley and felt warm again. I had to force my attention back to the meeting.

"So, we're going to pressure the mayor to set up a community meeting?" Joey asked, looking around the room for consensus.

People nodded. "A community meeting would give us a forum to state our case," Estelle added. "We're going to need that."

"We don't want the fate of the trees to be in the hands of some behind-closed-doors committee," agreed Elfreda.

Estelle pointed her long bony finger into the air. "Perhaps we should deluge the council with phone calls. Swamp them with petitions and letters. Let them know we're not going to permit such an injustice."

"Petitions are old hat," Joey said.

"The town must get dozens," Agatha argued.

Seeing Estelle's enthusiasm deflate, I came to the rescue. "We're not all going to agree about how to do this campaign. We're all going to have our own ideas. And why shouldn't we? Instead of trying to push everyone else into thinking like us, which is how they do it out there, let's support each other in going with our own impulses. So, if Estelle wants to head up a Deluge Campaign, all power to her. Go for it, Estelle. Whoever else likes that idea can join her. Are there others who want to work on that?" Seeing Grace's hand go up, I nodded. "There you go. Our first committee."

"If we do get a public meeting," Agatha said, "Boyd will present an open-and-shut case. They'll have the best legal advice and if they're smart, which they are, let's make no bones about that, they'll present an alternative tree-planting scheme to make it look as if nobody will lose anything. They're going to try to make us look like a bunch of doddering old fools. And if we're not careful, that's exactly what we will look like."

"And because we're women," added Joey strongly, "they'll say we're being emotional and irrational."

"As if we haven't heard that before!" Estelle laughed.

"At least they can't blame it on PMS!" Elfreda's face lit up. "Maybe it's PSS. Pre-senility syndrome!"

Agatha carried on amongst the chuckles. "What do we have to counter with? Some nostalgic testimonials about why the trees should stay? That's not much to fight back with." Grimly, the group considered her words.

"Maybe we should hire a lawyer," Grace suggested.

"Are there any older women lawyers in this town?" I asked.

"You kidding?" Joey chomped her teeth together.

"We've got to go it alone." Elfreda's tone was adamant. "The law's on their side anyway. If we play by their rules, we'll fall flat on our faces. We've got to fight it our own way."

"The trick," I said, thinking aloud, "will be to get a big wave of public support. Strong and vocal enough that the mayor and the town councillors will have to listen. And we need a forum for that. That's why we need a public meeting. Then they'll have to listen." Feeling all eyes on me, I carried on. "So, at the very least, we've got to broadcast what's been happening. Tell every person in Muskoka what Boyd is trying to do and what it's going to take to stop him."

Robyn's eyes widened.

"Yes!" Joey hit her corpulent thigh with her fist.

"How about a flyer?" Estelle suggested quietly.

"Yes. A flyer!" others agreed.

"We can put it under people's windshield wipers at the mall."

"And take it door to door."

"I could hand it out with the petition," Estelle added.

"Who wants to design it?" Elfreda threw the idea into the air and waited for someone to grab it.

"Robyn, I remember those wonderful posters you used to do for school," Agatha said. "Would you do it?"

I watched Robyn tense and hunch her shoulders. Agatha had always been generous with her and I didn't think my daughter would want to displease her.

Normally, I wouldn't have wanted Robyn to displease her either. Well-brought-up children were polite and accommodating. Well-brought-up children gave way to what others wanted. That's how I'd raised Robyn, as self-annihilating as that now seemed.

"Do whatever you want, Robyn," I said. If I wanted to find out who Robyn was, I had to support her right to make decisions on her own.

Robyn shot a doubtful glance my way. "Maybe," she said to Agatha. "I'll think about it."

"Hey, everybody," Elfreda announced. "There's some awfully cute guys coming up the driveway." All the Grannies stood up to look.

"I'll take the one with the hunky shoulders." Joey blew a big bubble with her gum.

"No, the blond one," Grace murmured, clasping her hands together in excitement. "Look at the size of his camera!"

Joey leaned forward to get a look at the camera which was hanging a few inches above his belt. "He's sure got a big one," she chuckled. "But it hangs a bit high – "

"Joey!" Agatha tried to sound indignant, but she, too, was smiling.

"I feel like I'm having a second childhood," Estelle said, an unusual lilt in her formal British voice.

"I feel like I'm having a first," Agatha stated, as she rose regally to greet the newsmen.

Chapter 8

The great Canadian melt was over. For weeks I'd been watching the huge frozen shoulders of snow that sulked along the roadsides melt into cool ponds for children to play in. As the days passed, the ground became squishy under my feet and the air took on the thick, fecund smell of decaying leaves and thawing dog droppings.

As spring erupted around me, I felt as restless as a teenager. Whenever I wasn't working on the tree-saving campaign or seeing clients, I bolted from the confines of my house into the open air. Like a waiting lover, the warm weather wrapped its arms around me and danced me into its soul-stirring fever. I wanted to run away from my life and stay outside forever.

Trees captivated me. I had always loved trees, but a new passion for them took root inside me. I noticed them wherever I went. And strange as it may sound, trees seemed to notice me in return. I first became aware of this as I was coming out of the library one day. As I walked, I had the distinct feeling that someone was looking at me. I turned, but there wasn't a person in sight. All I could see was a grand old pine tree. I had the distinct impression that it was aware of me.

Not something I would discuss with my colleagues.

They'd really think I'd gone crazy. And maybe I had. Lately I'd been having fantasies about taking one or two of my therapist friends out to the woods. I wanted to sit them down in the forest and let them feel the healing energies of trees.

All my training had taught me to separate people from their environment and treat them as psychological entities. Not only had I been taught to separate people from nature, but also to separate people's minds from their bodies and attend to their psychological processes as if this were a realm unto itself.

Nearly every book in my copious library instructed me, as a therapist, to help people just by talking to them, by working with what goes on inside their heads. The problem was, I no longer believed this way of working could heal. At least, not completely.

I wished Rudi were available. She could have helped me sort this out, for I wasn't sure I fully understood it yet. All I knew was that ever since the night in the park with the trees, I'd seen things differently. I didn't believe I was separate anymore. So I couldn't operate as if I were separate or treat others as if they were separate.

I imagined putting a bag made of cheesecloth in a stream. Could I heal what was inside that bag if I did not consider the state of the water that was constantly moving through it? Not likely. So, how could I help myself or anyone else to heal without bringing nature into the equation? I didn't think I could.

Clara, a client of mine, made the situation clearer to me. During her therapy, Clara had worked hard, but what finally cracked the stronghold of her depression was a two-week canoe trip in the wilderness. Those rocks and woods taught her things about life I never could. I don't want to play down what I did, for I know my work with her was helpful, I just don't think she would have ever truly healed without nature's involvement.

No wonder I was having so much difficulty concentrating when I was with clients. I wanted to take them out into nature. I wanted them to feel the smoothness of lilac leaves and experience the smell of cedar trees. I wanted them to hear the symphony of sound that goes on in a forest. And, I wanted to be out there with them.

Interestingly, Robyn had started work at a garden centre. Sometimes, when I went to pick her up, I sat in the car and watched her moving around amongst the plants and trees. I liked seeing her surrounded by green. I was envious that she worked so closely with nature. When she came home at night, she was physically exhausted. Often I'm tired from my day, but it's seldom a physical tiredness. I would have liked more physical tiredness. Maybe that would have helped me deal with my feelings about Harley.

I couldn't stop thinking about him. Over and over again, I saw his naked body on the rock that night we went swimming. Over and over again, I imagined myself being held by him, kissed by him. These imaginings were so real that once or twice I felt a moistness between my legs.

Sometimes I'd see him. Or think I had. A few times when I went out walking in the woods, I saw the shape of someone up ahead. The solid, broad-shouldered shape of Harley. I quickened my pace, but each time the figure seemed to vanish as if it had simply stepped into the trunk of a tree. Strange though, because the feeling of him being close remained.

At night my dreams were filled with trees. Often I dreamt I was flying over acres of green forests, my palms sliding along the leaf tops. Beneath me I could hear thousands of leaves rustling and swishing in the wind. One night I dreamt I was standing against a beech tree, my breasts pressed into its wide, rounded trunk. Its bark was smooth to my fingers, stretched tight around its turgid body. As I leaned against it, I felt myself being pulled into its towering height, my own bones and muscles attenuating like gum, elongating into slender branches that burst into fragile leaflets. My feet burrowed into the warm soil, digging past rocks and wet places, dividing and dividing until I had a thousand long toes rooted in the guts of the earth. A timeless peace filled my body with a sweetness like sap.

When I was near Candelabra, I felt the tree pressing itself towards me, as if it knew its survival was being threatened. I caught myself whispering comforting words to it when no one was looking. Was this part of menopause, imagining that trees were feeling anxious and comforting them? *Crazy old lady.*

Rudi. I needed to talk to her. She, if anyone, would understand. Hoping I wasn't becoming a pest, I telephoned again. Again her daughter answered. No, Rudi still wasn't well enough to take calls. Politely, I left my regards and rang off, but inside I felt like a small child denied access to her mother. Who else could I talk to? Harley. I wanted to talk to Harley. I looked for his number in the telephone book, but it was not there.

"Harley," I whispered, "I need you."

Meanwhile, like a closet psychic, I kept my communings with trees to myself. Which was easy to do, given how busy I was. Every day the tree campaign added a dozen new tasks to my schedule. Agatha had organized an extensive telephone scheme to persuade the town councillors to allow a general meeting. The other Grannies and I had each pledged to make ten phone calls a day. This meant that I had to phone ten people and convince them to get involved enough to contact a politician.

I had just finished my last call when the doorbell rang. It was Elfreda. The lines on her face had deepened, making her face look cracked and broken.

"Got some time?"

"Sure," I said, waving her into the living room. She stepped forward, then stopped and threw herself into my arms. She felt as small as a child, all bones and fragility.

"All I want to do this morning is drink," she said, pulling away and sinking into a chair. Charlie, his tail swishing with happiness, pressed his thick body into her legs. Leaning forward, she nuzzled her face into his with deep affection.

"I was wondering how you were doing with that."

"I didn't think it was going to be so hard," she said. "It's like walking through brambles – naked."

"Can you let the hurt out?" She looked at me dubiously, but I carried on. "If you can move it through you, you won't have to keep drinking it down."

"Drinking's easier," she whispered. Then she dropped forward, hiding her face in her hands.

I could see her struggling to hold back the tears. My heart went out to her. "It's all right to cry, Elfreda. Really," I said softly.

Bent forward, her body was bouncing slightly now, as she held back her emotions. As I watched her quietly, I could see the small bumps of her spine beading up through her sweater like a string of odd-sized pearls. Gently, I went over to her and put my hand on her shoulder. My touch seemed to spring something free, for suddenly she was crying, sobbing into her hands. I stroked her back as she cried. Her body felt hot.

"So silly," she muttered between short gasps of breath.

"It's fine," I soothed. "Just fine . . . "

My words allowed her to let ago again and she cried for a few more minutes. "It was like someone dumped a load of horse manure on me," she finally said, fighting for breath. "Taking them both like that. So close."

Elfreda leaned towards me and I massaged her shoulders. The muscles felt tight and ropy. I remembered back to how hard it had been losing Bart. Yet Elfreda had lost her husband and her child in the same year. I could only imagine how much that would hurt.

"And now they're trying to take away the trees." Her voice cracked with anger. "One of the few things worth being sober for." Reaching for a tissue, she blew her nose loudly.

I smiled. "Who would have thought that an elf of a thing like you could make such a noise blowing her nose!"

Elfreda chuckled. "Edward, my husband used to say that too. He used to call me Elfy." She looked at me shyly. "You could call me that, if you like."

"I would like," I said. "It sounds more like you."

Relieved that her upset was over, Charlie began licking Elfy's hand. "Oh, Charlie, what would I do without you, eh?" she crooned and put her arms around him. Smiling, she blew her nose again and sat up. "Life sure sucks sometimes."

"That it does," I said, standing up. "Would you like a cup of tea?" She nodded and in a few minutes, I brought two steaming cups back into the living room.

"It was hard when Edward went, but since he'd been sick, I was sort of prepared. But when Susan died, it was like someone robbed me of part of my body."

I thought about Robyn.

As if reading my mind, Elfreda asked, "I've been meaning to ask – how's Robyn? Is she settling down?"

I paused. As always, I seemed to have to gather my energy to talk about Robyn. "She's working . . . I'm trying to convince myself that means she might stay for awhile. But things still feel very precarious." I swallowed.

Elfy's eyes were sympathetic. "Susan got really pesky at that age too. I think it's because they're trying to launch themselves away from us and into their own lives and don't know how to do it. They need some grit for their feet to push against. Unfortunately, mothers make good grit." She was thoughtful for a moment. "And besides, when they're truly obnoxious, we stop holding on and start pushing from our end. That helps get them on their way, too."

She looked at me seriously, hesitated, then said, "Did something happen to Robyn? She looks wounded somehow."

"Does she?" My voice sounded casual, but a raddled lump of emotion formed in my throat. I reached for my tea to buy myself some time. If I could change the subject, there was a chance I could go on without crying, but I knew Elfy was on to me. I watched my finger go around and around the rim of my cup, then took a breath and pushed the words out.

"Robyn was raped."

Elfy groaned as if the words had hit her physically.

"I don't know all that happened," I continued, my throat still aching. "It was years ago now, before she went away, but from what I do know, it wasn't one of those horror stories. Her life wasn't threatened or anything. I don't even know if she fought back."

"As if that mattered," Elfy commented wryly. "When someone robs a bank, no one ever asks if the person fought back."

"You make it sound so simple."

"Do I? Maybe others just make it sound so complicated."

I nodded but said, "I was away when it happened. Bart found out, but the two of them decided not to tell me." I swallowed. "It was strange, because, when I came back home, I knew something had happened. Knew it in my body. I even remembered dreaming about something being wrong." I sipped the last of my tea. "It's funny that you used the word 'rob' a minute ago, because just before I found out about the rape, I dreamt that Robyn had been robbed. And that Bart was trying to bury something. The dream unsettled me for weeks. I couldn't figure it out. Not until after."

I remembered that night as if it had been burnt into my body. The words, the famous words, "Robyn, is there anything wrong?" And Robyn's eyes flashing to her father, who sat implacably reading the newspaper.

Trying to make it easier for her, I coached, "Perhaps a problem with a friend? Or some difficulty at school?" I knew sixteen was not an easy age.

Robyn's eyes, full of violent hurt, had grabbed mine, then tore themselves away as she ran to her room.

Reeling with confusion, I rose to go after her. Bart's whisper stopped me. "We weren't going to tell you," he said, his voice hermetic and dead. "Thought we'd spare you." He was silent for a moment. Then, speaking slowly, as if his carefulness would make the information less harsh, he told me the rest.

"Robyn was taken advantage of. It happened on the day she went birding. You were away and she was out on the escarpment looking for a particular flicker. I forget the name of it. Apparently a man had been watching her. He . . ." Bart cleared his throat. "He forced himself on her. But he didn't hurt her. At least, not physically. That's what she said."

The pain gathering in my chest made it hard to breathe. I forced my voice to talk. It sounded hoarse and raspy. "That was months ago. Why wasn't I told?"

Bart avoided my eyes. "Because we thought, I thought, it would be best for Robyn to forget about it. Neither she nor I wanted you to be hurt. And I thought she'd been through enough."

"She was raped for God's sake!" I shouted. I had never shouted at Bart before. "The police should have b– "

"Robyn did not want to involve the police. That she was sure about. She was frightened enough as it was."

Frantically, I ransacked back through the days to the night in question. I had come home late but had checked both children. Ted was studying and Robyn had her light out. I remembered thinking that it was early for Robyn to be sleeping, but I thought the outing had been more tiring than expected. The next day had been a school day and the routines had prevailed, as usual, steam-rolling everything into functional flatness.

Suppressing an impulse to retch, I left Bart and went to Robyn's room. I found Robyn lying on bed, face down, pretending to be asleep.

"And I let her pretend," I told Elfy, shame flooding my face. "I let her pretend."

As I talked, I felt my body sink down into the welter of despair that always awaited me when I allowed myself to think about that night.

"Then I climbed the Candelabra tree and cried my heart out."

Elfy held my hand in both of hers.

"I wanted her to press charges, of course, but Robyn wouldn't hear of it. She wouldn't talk about it to anyone, least of all, me. That's the part I don't get. Why she would never talk about it." I sighed. "After that, she went to Europe. Took the small inheritance her uncle left her and disappeared. Didn't write. Most of the time I didn't even know where she was. It was months after Bart's heart attack before I was able to reach her. She finally wrote, but she didn't come back. All I wanted was for her to come home so we could sort things out."

I blew my nose. "Now that she is back, I can't get her to talk about any of it. Here I thought this was going to be our opportunity to make things better. To get close. But emotionally she might as well be in Siberia. I'm worried that she's going to take off again." Tears of hopelessness pooled in my eyes. "She might leave and we'll still have all this unfinished business."

Elfy passed me a tissue. "One thing is certain – she's not going to deal with it if she isn't ready. But she must be close or she wouldn't have come home."

I shook my head. "Just once I'd like to get to the centre

of things with Robyn. Instead of getting lost in the shadows."

"Well, if she's watching you, it shouldn't take long."

"What do you mean?"

"You're so on target with your own life, that's got to rub off a little, don't you think?"

"I hope so," I said. We sat together quietly for awhile and I felt myself calm. It felt good to have Elfy sitting beside me.

Hearing a tap at the window, we both looked up and saw Grace's cheerful face in my window. She was holding a newspaper and pointing to something on the front page.

As if on cue, both Elfy and I strained forward. I heard the breath catch in Elfy's throat. There, on the front page was a photograph of me, Elfy and the Grannies. Elfy and I blew our noses and grinned like kids.

Chapter 9

The newspaper article hit the stands and exploded like a bomb in my living room. The phone began ringing and kept on ringing. Calls came from people who wanted to help with the campaign, from newspapers and from radio stations. Since Agatha had appointed herself Chief Public Relations Officer, I passed these calls on to her.

Over the next few weeks, Agatha proved herself to be an organizational genius. She sent out press releases, contacted media people and commandeered interviews with the efficiency of a company president.

Things were still hopping when the day came for me to take Luke to the powwow. There was so much to do in the campaign that I thought about asking Ted to get another sitter for Luke, but I didn't want to let either of them down. Besides, I wanted to go to the powwow. Would I see Harley there?

As I dressed, I wondered about Madge. Would she show up? We had made an arrangement for her to come to the powwow weeks ago, but since then she'd broken a few of our race-walking dates, so I wasn't sure if I'd see her. I wasn't sure I even wanted to see her.

Hearing a car honk, I went outside to greet Ted and Luke. I could tell Ted was in a hurry by the way he stood by the car, obviously anxious to get on with his business trip.

"Catch up with you on the way back," he said, kissing my cheek warmly. He nodded towards Luke. "Don't let him run you ragged." He grinned as if knowing this was a silly thing to say, waved and went off.

Inside the house, Luke threw his small arms around me, then dropped to his knees to pat Charlie who was quivering with eagerness.

I sat beside them, watching my grandson play with the dog. A warm, satisfied feeling came into my chest. There's nothing like family, I thought. It was as if my bones took comfort knowing that blood that was my own was near.

Funny, I thought, to be held together by this strange container called family. Each generation creates its own mixture, shaped by the heat and pressures of the times, expanding with each birth, contracting with each death, moving forward like a vast amoebic force, on and on through the eons.

"Hi, Aunt Madge!" Luke called as Madge came through the door. He poked his head to the side, trying to get a glimpse of what Madge was holding behind her back.

"Something to keep your mouth occupied," Madge explained, her red lips smiling. She handed him a bag of gummi bears, then tossed a small packet my way.

Fudge. I loved fudge and Madge knew it. My first impulse was to hurl it back at her. But I made myself smile, accepting the gift as the peace offering it was. Gathering my things, I felt relieved, but not relaxed. Maybe spending the day with Madge would do us both good. Maybe it would give us enough time to open up to each other again. But how did you open up to someone you didn't trust?

I snuck a sidelong glance at her as she sat with Luke.

Usually I liked her bright clothes, but this morning they seemed like a neon sign saying, "Look at me, look at me!" I felt as if I were looking at a narcissistic teenager, someone who would do anything, sacrifice whatever was necessary to have these "me" needs met. This scared me. What about my needs? What about the needs of our friendship?

I knew from my work that inside all of us is a variety of what I call "subpersonalities" which vie for attention. The process of living has a way of calling some of these aspects onto centre stage every once in a while. The threat to the trees, for example, had brought the part of me that's an ecological radical out into the open. Middle-age was bringing out Madge's teenager. The problem was that teenagers and tree-huggers don't have very much in common.

Luke, who had skipped down into the basement to say a quick hello to Robyn, came running back up. "Can Robyn come? I already asked her and she says she wants to."

"Sure," I answered, thinking the day might provide us all with some much needed distraction.

Robyn came upstairs and stopped at the sight of Madge. "Oh – I didn't know you were coming . . ."

"Yes, ma'am," Madge said, offering Luke a candy.

I looked from Robyn to Madge. What was going on between these two? I sighed. *Why is everything so complicated these days?* The four of us got into the car.

We drove for a while with none of us speaking. Only Luke made any sounds and those were the zaps and boofs of two army toys he was playing with in the back seat.

I felt awkward beside Madge, not knowing what to say. Wasn't she going to ask me anything about the tree campaign? Surely she'd seen the articles and the photographs? Was she really going to carry on as if nothing had happened? We turned down the road leading to the reserve.

"Funny," Madge said finally, "this Indian reservation is so close, but I've never been in before." She scanned the landscape. "For some reason, I thought the houses would look more dilapidated."

I nodded, looking around as I drove. The houses tended to be small, some brick, but most with wood siding. They looked like the houses of people still struggling with the basics.

The house we were passing now had a large vegetable patch in front and standing in the middle of it, working the soil, was an old woman wearing a red scarf. The very image of her brightened my spirits. I'd heard of so much tragedy from life on the reserve. Alcoholism, violence, suicide – not surprising, given the way Indians had been stripped of their culture and integrity. But still, it hurt me to hear of people getting beaten up, or jailed, or having to cut the rope from around some child's broken neck.

Madge stared at the old woman. "Ever get a chance to talk to Elfreda?"

"As a matter of fact I did. She's on the wagon, for the moment anyway. Being involved in the tree campaign has helped a lot."

"That won't last." Madge fidgeted with her blood-red fingernails.

When had Madge started painting her nails? The colour made them look brazen and ravenous. I imagined them drawing blood on a man's back.

"I don't think people can change like that," she added.

"Of course they can." Outrage pricked at my skin. "I've worked with people who have turned their lives around 180 degrees. People debilitated with phobias or anxiety – "

"What's a phobia, Gran?"

"It's when a person has an unreasonable fear of something."

"Like I do, of heights," Madge admitted.

"Do you have a wrang like my gran does with snakes?"

"A wrang?" Madge questioned. "Is that close to a hairy?"

"A wrang. A hairy. A bird. You name it, I have it," I admitted.

"Aren't you embarrassed, mother?" Robyn's voice was cool. "Being a therapist and having a fear like that?"

I felt as if I were standing in the middle of a firing range. "Most people have something they're afraid of. Therapists are just people, like everybody else." I tried to sound open and vulnerable despite my tension. If I wanted Robyn to be vulnerable, I was going to have to lead the way. "At least, what I'm afraid of doesn't get in the way of things. I mean, how often do I run into a snake?"

"I'm not afraid of anything," Luke said.

I replayed the scene: the long green ribbon of snake lacing through the grass. Me, three years old, running after it, playing with it, letting it coil around my arm. My mother coming out. Screaming. Screaming. Then dropping. A lifeless body. My brother beating the snake with a stick until it, too, was dead.

"Don't you touch a snake again or I'll drop dead for real next time," my mother warned, coming out of her faint.

Fears. In my years as a psychotherapist, it always amazed me the way they burrowed down into a person's cells, especially in the loamy soil of childhood. And once a fear took root, it usually grew into the person's adulthood, strengthening with each passing year.

"What's a powwow?" Luke asked, pulling me into the present.

"I'm not really sure," I said. "I think it's some sort of gathering. Or celebration, maybe. I think the Indians are trying to find out who they are again. Maybe these get-togethers help them to do that. Reconnect them with their traditions."

Madge nodded, yawning hugely.

"Too many late nights?" I almost asked, but bit my tongue. Just yesterday, Donna, the client Boyd had dumped a few months ago, told me she'd gone out with him "for a drink". Whatever that meant. Knowing Donna, it could mean the whole shooting match. Some people only know stop or go, nothing in between. Was the bastard seeing both of them? And what about Donna? Was she prepared to jeopardize her relationship with Doug for a fling with Boyd?

I wished I could tell Madge about Donna but I couldn't. What I could tell her was what happened the night in the park with Boyd. That might wake her up a bit. Then I realized it wouldn't wake her up at all, because she wouldn't believe me.

Ahead, a long line of cars appeared at the side of the road and people were emerging out of them and crossing to a field where a large tent was set up.

"Look!" Luke screamed. "Tepees!"

There, beyond the parking area, was a huge tepee with

a large, yellow sun painted on the side. Another smaller one was decorated with an intricate zigzag pattern in red and black, others were covered with drawings of animals.

Luke ran into one, his legs leaping delightedly at the secluded space inside. "Can I have one? Can I?"

"These wouldn't be for sale, honey," Madge said.

"You could probably make one," I offered. "Use some branches and old sheets."

Luke was out of the tepee now and looking at the various wares being sold at the stalls around the big tent: moccasins, beadwork, blankets, stone carvings, braids of sweetgrass, miniature birch-bark canoes.

"Oh, I like this." I pointed to a hand-sized ring of leather. Inside the ring was an intricate web of woven thread.

"It's a dream catcher," said the woman behind the table.

"The web part must catch the dreams," Madge surmised. "You should give these to your clients."

I surveyed them more closely. Many had been painted neon pink or iridescent blue.

"Tacky colours," Madge whispered. "They look like they belong in the CNE."

"I wish they could have left them the natural leather colour," I agreed quietly. But the native woman must have heard because I felt her staring at us with hard eyes.

I grimaced. It really wasn't fair. We expected natives to hold on to what was natural when we couldn't do that ourselves. We didn't support them in living their way of life, yet when they tried to do their thing our way, we complained that it had no soul.

Madge moved with Robyn to a booth selling baskets

while Luke and I meandered in the direction of the big tent. As we walked, children darted past, weaving their way through the various clumps of people that arranged and rearranged themselves around the craft tables. The thundering of the drum in the big tent grew louder.

Feeling something pulling at me, I turned to see Harley Skinkeeper's eyes. "Our friend again," whispered Madge from behind, as if to warn me. But my body already knew. The bowl of my pelvis was already filling with warmth.

Harley was arranging a band of beads on a honey-coloured leather hat he'd made. Quickly, he etched a lone pine on the side of the hat, then reached forward and placed it gently but firmly on my head.

I smiled self-consciously and tried not to blush. I liked the feel of it very much. It seemed to hold me down closer to the earth.

"He's giving it to her!" Luke said. "How come?"

No one spoke. Harley held my eyes peacefully. My face became hot.

"I guess he likes her," Madge said.

The drumming in the big tent sounded very loud and I could feel it pulsing inside my body. When I ventured another look at Harley, he was working on some moccasins. I watched him, aware of the intensity of my body's reaction.

It was his wildness that drew me. I was aware of it, even from a distance. It emanated from his body like the aroma of an animal. Not a fierce, predatory kind of wildness, but the kind that knows the smell of wet stones picked fresh from a stream, the feel of moss on a bare back, the taste of the wind in mountains. It was as though this man's body flowed in the same river of movement that made the planets dance and wolves howl. For the first time in my life, I felt the imperative of having this wildness move through me too. Unconsciously, my body swayed towards him, as if it could feed on the juice of him.

"I want this," Luke said, putting on a leather hat with a snakeskin band.

An older man stood up. He wore a snakeskin vest over a frayed yellow sweater that barely covered his protruding belly. One of his eyes was damaged and the pupil was rolled up so just the white could be seen below the drooping eyelid.

"This is Felix," Harley said, introducing his friend.

"Where'd you get the snakeskin?" Luke asked.

"From the snake," the man growled, staring at Luke with one grizzly eye. Then, jerking his head to the side in a gesture that Luke understood, he turned abruptly and Luke followed him over to a rusty van parked beside the stall.

Harley looked at me, his dark eyes as open as a pair of outstretched arms.

Elated, Luke returned a few minutes later. "He's got this huge snake in there. Says I can hold it sometime. I'm not afraid," he assured the old man. "My gran, she's afraid of snakes." I returned the old man's look, but not easily. His one eye was too powerful to stare at for long.

"Wow!" Luke's attention locked on to a man dressed in a wolf skin headdress who was walking towards the big tent. The wolf skin was positioned on the man's head so that the wolf's nose jutted out between his eyes, its forelegs splaying over the forehead and down by each ear. It looked as if the animal were holding the man's head in its grasp.

The man wore honey-coloured moccasins with an anklet of bells that tinkled with every step.

"Wow!" Luke turned to follow. The old man repossessed the hat from Luke's head as he passed and Robyn, always watchful of Luke, followed.

I pulled my eyes away from Harley. My thighs tingled as they used to when I was a child and about to mount a horse. Taking Madge's arm, I led her towards the main tent.

"Can't take it, eh?" Madge could smell an infatuation like an ant a picnic.

"I'll take Harley and you take Felix," I quipped.

"Yeah, that Felix is a real turn-on." She burst into laughter, her mouth as wide as a poppy.

I pushed us forward into the tent. In the middle of the space was a line of big-bellied drums two or three feet wide. Around the drums sat a half dozen men, each holding wooden beating sticks. The men in the group nearest us threw down their cigarettes, lifted their drum beaters and hit them thunderously against the drums. A roaring, rhythmic drumming began, and the men, eyes closed and mouths open, began to make a high-pitched, eerie sound. "Aiyeeeeeee, iiiieeeeeee . . ."

"What're they saying?" Luke shouted over the sound.

I shrugged, unsure. Around us, people began to dance. Children in outfits of red and yellow sequins danced beside women in dresses jingling with hundreds of conical bells. Many of the men wore buckskin jackets decorated with feathers, beads and wool.

The music stopped. Everyone looked towards a man holding a wooden staff that had been carved into the shape of an otter's head with two delicate antlers.

Speaking first in his native tongue, then English, in a tone as reverent as though God were beside him listening, he said, "Oh, Great Spirit, Great Father of the four winds, light of light, the voice of the whispering trees, hear my prayers."

After the prayer, the drumming and singing began again, this time with even greater intensity. I felt my body vibrating.

"I'm going to find Luke," I told Madge. Wandering around the food stalls, I caught a glimpse of him over near Harley's booth. Quickly, I moved through the crowd until I was a few feet behind him.

Worried I'd lose him again, I reached out to grasp Luke's collar, but what my hand grabbed was slippery. It came away from his collar and moved up my arm. To my horror, the head of it was in my hands. The blood left my face, then my lungs could no longer pull air and as my body slipped to the ground, the words in my throat became a hiss, a hiss as soft and unheard as the hiss in the throat of the snake I was somehow holding.

Then there was air, great gulps of sweet air and I felt a friend come close. When I opened my eyes, Harley's hands were on my shoulders.

"She's awake," Madge's worried face leaned towards me.

"Gran!" Luke ran to the other side of me.

Using them as supports, I pulled myself up. The one-eyed man sat calmly a few feet away, the offending reptile coiled easily in his lap.

"It wouldn't have hurt you," Luke assured me fervently, casting a reverent look towards the old man. "The old guy's been teaching me about him. He let me hold him, let me walk around with him on my neck."

I tried to talk, but my voice had been swallowed by my fear. Luke looked at me and smiled. I was glad he could enjoy the snake. The last thing I wanted was to pass my fear along to others, as had been done to me.

The old man, his eyes closed, began to speak softly but fervently in his native tongue.

Madge nudged Harley. "What's he saying?"

"He's saying that Snake Medicine is powerful," Harley explained. "Medicine means the teaching of Snake. Its Wisdom. He says Snake knows when to leave the old behind. Snake is telling her to let go. Follow her instincts. He says Snake came to her before. Now he comes again. Same message. More important now. Snake is not afraid of what others think. He is telling her to leave fear behind. Take it off. Like Snakeskin. Begin new life. New life calls."

I looked from the man to the snake. He wasn't restraining it. Like a pet, it sat quietly in his lap, eyes open, looking at me. Inside, two forces pulled. The one from the past churned my stomach like a tyrant and told me to run. The other, the newer and healthier part, simply regarded the snake inquisitively, knowing there was nothing to be afraid of. For a moment the two forces battled, then like a deep sigh, the fear left and I relaxed.

Relieved as an animal released from a cage, I said, "I want to go home."

"Of course, you do," Madge crooned.

I turned to the two men. "Thank you." A bemused smile slipped over my lips. "It's been quite an experience."

Harley eased me up to my feet and set the hat back firmly on my head.

Chapter 10

In the days following the powwow, an unsettled yearning took over my body. I could feel it deep in the womb of me, growing up from my belly, through my chest and along my arms, making me want to reach out for things beyond what my current life offered.

Spring fever, I told myself. With a bit of Harley fever thrown in. Everyone is restless at this time of year in Canada. In the dead of winter, most of us are too frozen to feel anything, but once we sniff warm weather, we get stirred into a froth of desire for new things. All I wanted was to take off my clothes and feel the sun on my naked skin. I craved heat from the marrow of my bones and began to hate the cold with the intensity of a hostage.

It helped to be busy with the tree campaign. Like the other Grannies, every day I spent time phoning people and writing letters. Each of us made six calls a day, which totalled up to hundreds every week. Our hope was that at least three-quarters of the people we called would contact the mayor and tell him to save the trees. Or tell him to call a community meeting. He had to listen to that many people, didn't he? Being election year, we were counting on it.

The Grannies jumped into the campaign like monkeys onto the vine. They were everywhere: in the supermarkets with petitions, in the streets talking with people, in the newspapers, on television and on radio. Not having the responsibilities of children or jobs, they had inordinate amounts of time and energy to devote to the campaign. When I kidded Joey one day, asking her if she ever slept, she said, "My usual five hours. But now if I can't sleep, I just don't twiddle my thumbs, I get up and write protest letters."

I smiled. Who would have thought that old people could be so tough, so tireless, so determined? My respect for the Grannies grew every day. Agatha continued to be a veritable bulldozer, ploughing through heaps of work and looking around for more. Estelle was relentless in the way she hounded people to sign her petition. Joey had a brutish tenacity that didn't quit and Grace, despite the gentleness she presented to the world, was as intrepid as the rest of them.

The person I enjoyed working with the most was Elfy. The ginger-haired old woman was as inexhaustible as the other Grannies, but Elfy took an impish delight in every aspect of the campaign. The tree crusade seemed to have released her from the weight of her grief. Without the dulling haze of alcohol, she became even more high-spirited and humorous.

One day, after I'd made my calls, I was taking Charlie for a walk when I heard a car honking and saw Elfy driving beside me.

"We did it!" she shouted, pulling the car up on the sidewalk and barely missing a fence.

"What? What did we do?"

Her eyes flashed like tossed coins. "The mayor's agreed to a public meeting. It must have been all those phone calls," she said breathlessly.

Relief bubbled through my chest. Now we had a chance.

That night, we all met for dessert and coffee at Basil's. Agatha ordered an expensive bottle of champagne to celebrate. She ordered Elfy some sparkling mineral water so her glass wouldn't look different from the others.

Cheeks flushed, Elfy stood up. She held a thick bag protectively to her chest. "Since I had a couple of hours between hearing about our victory and the meeting tonight, I thought I'd get us a little surprise." She paused a moment for dramatic impact. "Now close your eyes."

I could hear rustling sounds, then Elfy sang, "Ta da!"

When I opened my eyes, Elfy was standing in front of us with her arms held out victoriously. She was wearing a tee-shirt with a beautiful photograph of the Candelabra tree printed in colour on the front.

"How lovely," Estelle murmured, turning to Joey, who nodded approvingly.

Elfy spun around and there, on the back, was printed in big, bold letters: GUERRILLA GRANNY.

Agatha groaned, but the rest of us cheered.

"I got one for everybody." Elfy pulled more shirts from the bag and tossed them to people. Agatha left hers unfolded on her lap, but the rest of us pulled them on over our clothes like kids playing dress-up.

"Where'd you get the wonderful photograph?" I asked.

"It's one of Robyn's," Elfy told me happily.

"Those weren't for general consumption." Agatha frowned. "They were for the flyer."

"Sorrrrreeee." Elfy waved her hand in the air as if she were recovering from a slap on the knuckles.

With a martyred expression on her face, Agatha spoke.

"As you know, I asked Robyn to do a flyer for us. Knowing what an extraordinary photographer Robyn was in high school, I asked if she could do the flyer using photographs. I thought photographs of the trees would make the poster more alive. How right I was!" She held up some of the enlargements. The group hushed.

"My word," Estelle said. "She's made the trees look regal."

Joey whistled loudly.

"Incredible," Elfy whispered.

I smiled, deeply pleased. The photographs proved beyond a doubt that Robyn had a deep and true love of trees. Maybe we weren't so different after all.

"I think you'll all agree," continued Agatha confidently, "the Candelabra photograph is the most breathtaking. So, that's the one we chose for the flyer." She held up the flyer for all to see.

"Wonderful."

"Superb."

Agatha acknowledged the praise and carried on. "Now that we have the public meeting to advertise, we can print up a few thousand with the date of the meeting right on it."

The Grannies sat spellbound.

"There's more," Agatha announced. "I took the photographs to Estelle's son, who as you know, has his own printing business. He's put them together into a calendar." She held a sample of the calendar for all to see. "There's a different tree for each month." As she turned the pages, everyone "oohhed" and "ahhhed."

"I thought we could sell it as a fund-raiser, which should be particularly lucrative since Estelle's son has offered to do the printing free as a donation to our cause."

The group cheered Agatha loudly. Joey patted her heartily on the back.

When the applause had quietened, Estelle stood up and gave her report on the petition. "What's extraordinary is that no one ever turns me down. All I have to do is ask someone to sign it and they do!" Her eyes bulged with wonderment.

"It's your accent," Grace said.

"Naw, it's that lavender talcum powder crap," Joey said. "She douses herself with the stuff. It's her secret weapon."

A look of merriment skimmed across Estelle's face, but she said nothing.

"I think people just like grannies," Elfy offered. "If they see a little old lady canvassing for something, they think it must be worth supporting."

"As it must," Joey said. "We're too old to care about anything that isn't important."

"We're just irresistible." An impish smile played on Agatha's mouth.

Joey guffawed loudly and tossed back the last of her champagne.

"Whatever the reason," Estelle said, "I now have over two thousand signatures."

Again, cheers resounded in the room. As everyone clapped, I noticed Elfy sipping a drink. Wasn't that Grace's glass she was drinking out of? A knot formed in my stomach.

Agatha stood up. "Just to bring you up to date on the media aspect: I've been contacted by eighteen newspapers and twelve radio stations. I've sent out over two hundred press releases and given twenty-one interviews." Agatha smoothed her expensive silk skirt and sat, accepting the tumultuous applause as if it were her due. From her chair, she concluded, "My goal in the next few weeks is to have every newspaper and magazine in Canada aware of our campaign."

"Whoa!" Joey said. "This lady doesn't fool around."

"Old geezers like us don't have time to fool around," Elfy said. "We have to make every moment count!"

Joey rubbed her thick hands together. "We've got them on the run now."

"Now that there's going to be a public meeting, what are we going to do with it?" asked Grace. "How are we going to get people to come?"

"Why don't we have a picnic in the park just before the meeting," I suggested, trying to get my mind away from Elfy. "That will get people out."

"Yes!" Elfy said. "A potluck dinner."

"With music and balloons," Grace added, getting enthused.

"I could get more people to sign my petition," Estelle said.

"And we could sell my calendars," Agatha said.

"Don't you mean *our* calendars?" Elfy said.

"Grace is right. We still have to decide what we're actually going to do at this meeting." Joey wrung her hands together. "Somebody's going to have to say something, aren't they?" She frowned. "You guys all know I'm in this one hundred percent, but don't ask me to talk. The very idea of it makes my knees shake. But someone's got to do it."

Almost in unison, the group turned and looked at me.

Elfy pointed a wrinkled finger at my face. "You're the most eloquent."

"I'm not old enough," I argued. Everyone laughed. "I'm not even a senior citizen."

"This isn't about pension cheques – it's about trees," Joey said.

"I'll think about it." At least, that was what I'd planned to say. The word that came out of my mouth was "Yes." Around me, everyone clapped. I gulped.

Agatha carried on. "No doubt each side will be given time to speak. The mayor, despite his antiquated ecological philosophy, is a gentleman, so we, as ladies, will probably be offered the first opportunity."

"Sexist bastard," Joey said.

Agatha arched an eyebrow and gave Joey a cold, piercing look. "Good manners, my dear, are a sign of good breeding." She smoothed her hair and continued. "Whatever the order of events, we had better prepare ourselves for the worst, because, unquestionably, Boyd's presentation is going to be the epitome of sophistication."

"If only there was some way of discrediting their case." Elfy's face became a mass of jumbled lines.

"A bomb scare," Joey quipped. "Down, Aggie. I was kidding."

Agatha quashed the suggestion anyway. "They'd just reschedule and we'd be blamed. That's not the kind of publicity we want."

I turned and whispered to Elfy. "I see that smile. What are you thinking?"

Elfy shrugged, unwilling to share her thoughts. But the puckish smile remained.

"I think we should have a bunch of presenters," Joey said. "Maybe start with some bigwig from the environmental movement, then have someone from the cottage association and finish with a foot-stomping speech by Jessie here."

"Right, load me up with expectations . . ." I moaned.

Elfy patted my leg. "Don't get your knickers in a knot, girl."

"I've got an interview in half an hour." Agatha began packing up her things. "Perhaps we can all think of ideas and discuss them at our next meeting." She reached into her briefcase. "Oh, I almost forgot, here's the new schedule," she said, handing out sheets of paper. From the day the trees had been threatened, the Grannies had set up a twenty-four-hour surveillance of the trees. They knew Boyd was capable of anything.

"No one is getting hassled, are they?" Joey asked. "Remember, we need to stay on the side of the park that belongs to the town. Then he can't touch us." Everyone nodded.

"I must go this minute." Agatha headed towards the door, waved and was gone. The others gathered up their things.

Elfy leaned towards me. "Want to come with us for some line dancing?"

I had to stop myself from sniffing her breath. "No, but thanks." I'd had a busy day with clients, followed by this meeting and I needed time to catch up with myself. Particularly now, since I'd committed myself to giving a speech.

The others went off together and I walked home. When I arrived back at the house, I was too restless to go inside, so I put the canoe in the lake. The water was a dance of a thousand ripples, light blue near the shore and silver and orange in the middle. I paddled down into the bay where the water was still. My canoe slid through the water as if through liquid air.

Above me, the sky was full of great billowy clouds in different shades of purple, grey and blue. After I'd paddled awhile, a light rain began to fall, making enormous dimples in the water out of which spun huge rippling rings that circled wider and wider.

Plonk. Plonk. I always liked the sound of rain on water. It was a soothing, joyful sound and it calmed me. To fend off the rain, I put on the hat Harley had given me, liking the warm, snug way it fit on my head. Other hats I'd owned had to be held down in a wind, but this was sturdy and protective and stayed with me. It smelled of animals and wild things, just like Harley. I liked that.

Zipping up my jacket, I paddled over to the old ones, my name for the grand cottages of decades past. These were the cottages people used to come to for the whole summer, bringing along an entourage of relatives and staff.

The one I was passing now was a classic, a rambling main cottage skirted with wide verandas on all three sides. I remembered playing there as a child, intrigued even then by the endless nooks and crannies of the place. A pantry, a kitchen with an old-fashioned Findlay stove, a play room with games like Sorry, Parcheesi, Clue, Checkers and Monopoly. All the rooms had been panelled in vertical honey-coloured pine slats, floor, walls and ceiling. And in the living room, there had been a magnificent grand piano, brought across the lake in the dead of winter when the ice was as thick as a coffin.

Paddling closer, I could smell the musty woodiness of the boathouse even now. Once upon a time, all the cottages in Muskoka had that rustic aroma. They were supposed to. Just as they were supposed to look a bit weathered and worn. That was part of their comfort. No one would have painted a dock white like the one I was paddling towards. White dock, white bench, bracketed at each end by two planters that would, no doubt, be filled with pink geraniums when the summer people arrived. Geraniums indeed! In my day, geraniums were considered far too city-like for the wilds of Muskoka. But the wilds of Muskoka, like most wild things, had left and headed farther north.

North. Up north. The words still rang in my body like a bell. In my youth, in the city, that's what we'd say: up north. *Where you going? Up north!* As if it were a definable place. Which was crazy given the size of Canada's northern regions. And absurd if one measured how far north Muskoka actually was. In terms of the vast body of Canada, Muskoka was just above the country's ankles. Yet people liked to think it was way up in the hinterland, rough and wild. As if thinking of it like that would bring some of the wildness their way.

Geographically, the words meant nothing. Yet, somehow, they were magic, conjuring up a myriad of sensations: the rock-reedy smell of the clear water, the awesome, whimsical flashing of the northern lights, the delicate feeling of the lake winds streaming through my hair. God's country. That's what my father whispered as we stood on the dock after the long drive from the city.

The cottages here were called summer homes now. Affordable to the rich only. Once there had been a special bay of cottages called Millionaire's Row. Now, many of the lakefront properties in Muskoka were in that price range. As I paddled, I could smell steak barbecuing. The rain had ended and hardy cottagers up for the weekend would be pouring vodka coolers while the Mammas and the Papas crooned over portable compact disc players. Some would be lolling about in hot tubs built right into the landscape. Others would be in their saunas. The good life. In Muskoka, it came with all the trimmings.

You'd think that all this loveliness would produce lovely people. People who listened to one another, who were respectful, who gave the best of themselves. But the men beat up their wives here, too. The only difference was that they wore Ralph Lauren shirts and appeased their guilt with Seagram's Five Star instead of a six pack.

My client, Donna, was from one of these "better" families. Her sex-abusing father had a cottage just around the corner. I'd met him at a dinner party once. I'd met Donna's ex-husband, too. He was an abusive man as well. Not physically, but constantly and brutally, he used to assault her with words.

The mutual attraction of the abuser and the abused was always a two-person dance. One might take the lead, but the other kept step.

I wondered how often Donna was seeing Boyd. Why would she even see someone who had dropped her so ruthlessly? Maybe she needed another round with Boyd to drive the lesson home. Sometimes people set themselves up in just such a way in order to get back on track again. Now, with Madge on the scene, it seemed inevitable that Donna was going to get hurt. Or Madge. Did Donna know about Madge? Did Madge know about Donna? This situation was sounding more like a soap opera every day. And where did Doug fit in to the picture?

I tried to think about Madge as if she were a client, knowing that would help me understand her and feel less angry. Many women, especially women who had relied on their good looks, began to feel a squeeze of desperation at mid-life. Men no longer whistled at them when they walked down the street. And old age was staring them in the face. I'd seen many women sidestep their terror of aging by throwing themselves into the arms of the most inappropriate men. It never worked, but sometimes, they had fun trying. At other times, they were damaged beyond repair.

I sighed. What Madge did was none of my business. Why was I thinking about her anyway? To distract myself, I paddled closer to the bay where the big trees were. From the water, they looked grand and wise.

When I was five, I saw a huge oak tree being felled. My parents told me I cried hysterically, certain that with nothing to hold them up, the clouds and stars would come tumbling down and we would all be squashed and burned. Shaking my head, as though to off-load the memory, I paddled towards the tranquillity of the trees. That's what I loved about trees the most. The way they brought me home to the quietness in my heart.

Above me, a huge limb curved down towards the water and I reached out and touched a tiny leaf bud that was about to spring open. I closed my eyes and felt my fingers tingle with the wildness in this one, small, curled-up leaf. I needed this wildness to stay sane. I needed this wildness to stay alive.

When were people going to understand that trees were

not a luxury but a necessity? That our survival and their survival were the same thing. "When you tell them," Rudi's voice answered inside me.

All right, Rudi. You'd better be as talkative when it's speech writing time. Rudi's daughter had told me yesterday that she was on a new medication and the doctors were hopeful she'd be fully recovered in a few days. Thank goodness for that. What the Grannies had asked me to do felt like such an awesome responsibility. The future of these trees might depend on it. I wanted Rudi's support.

Moving the canoe gently and silently through the water, I was revelling in the peacefulness of the evening when a fire-engine red speedboat came roaring towards me. The boat was one of those huge fibreglass fiascoes with more engine power than any small lake could contend with. I tensed as the boat zoomed towards me, veering away from collision at the last second. As it cut its engine, a gigantic wave rolled towards me and my canoe bobbed crazily.

As the boat idled closer, I imagined slamming the flat of my paddle against the surface of the water and splashing the people in the boat, whoever they were.

"Jess!" Taking off a scarf, Madge waved girlishly as the boat approached.

I stared at the woman in the canary yellow outfit as if I'd never seen her before. Boyd's face broke into a broad mannequin-like smile. He ran one hand expansively through his blond hair as though preening before a group of admirers. Dressed in white slacks and baby blue shirt, he had an expensive sweater knotted rakishly at the neck. He looked like a male model.

"We were just having a quickie boat ride before dusk," Boyd said.

Wrestling down my anger, I said nothing. I could feel Boyd's eyes on my face.

In a slow, calculated manner, he raised his arm and wrapped it around Madge's shoulders. "Get me another beer, will you?" Madge jerked her head towards him, then moved to the back of the boat where the cooler was.

Boyd leaned towards me with a thin smile and said quietly, "I'm going to win, you know."

I looked past Boyd to Madge. Who was this person sitting in Boyd's boat? She was certainly not the Madge I knew. Scarlet fingernails, tight yellow sweater.

"Maybe you deserve this guy after all," I said, looking into her eyes.

Boyd gunned the boat, sending a sudden wave of water that rocked my canoe wildly. It was all I could do to steady myself as their boat sped away.

I sat for a long time, not moving. Then, hearing a noise, I looked up. There, stretched above me in the sky, was a gigantic "V" of geese. I leaned backwards, listening to their honking. They were flying low enough that I could hear the steady whooshing of their pumping wings. They were coming home. Redeemed, I picked up my paddle and made my way back.

Chapter 11

Finally, it was the May 24th long weekend. Like most Canadians, I didn't mind if it was cold because I knew that summer was now owed to me. When I dropped Robyn off at the gardening centre, the place was crowded with cottagers buying bedding plants. They weren't concerned that a frost might send them out in their pyjamas to cover their little green babies with newspapers and empty margarine containers because the very fact that the plants were out meant that the warm weather was on its way. Buying bedding plants proved it, surely.

After buying a few trays of vegetable seedlings, I sat happily on a small hill overlooking my back garden. It was a large garden with several trees, sloping gracefully down to the lake. Beneath me, I could feel the cool, wet grasses poking up into my skin and a wild tingling sensation arising out of the earth. I felt the very organisms in the soil were whooping it up in some impassioned spring ritual. A breeze, smooth as a bird's flight, winged by my face. As if to catch it, I sucked in some air, sweet and wet, and held it in my lungs. It felt so alive, fluttering with the embryonic heartbeats of baby summer moons, corn cobs and peaches.

I needed a morning off from the avalanche of details I'd been caught in since the tree campaign had started. For days I had been planning the agenda of the public meeting, contacting people who might make financial contributions to the campaign, helping distribute the flyer and talking to reporters. But today I knew I had to detach myself from all of that and come back to the simple things – the cool, wet feel of soil in my hands, the smell of pine needles, strong and spicy after the mortar and pestle of winter ice.

As I sat in the early morning sun, the tiredness of the last few days left me. Robyn was away working, then going off to a friend's overnight, so I had today and part of tomorrow to myself. The only person I was going to see was Elfy, who'd promised to come over and show me what to do. This was my first vegetable garden and I wanted to do it right.

The problem was, I kept thinking about Harley. Luscious, lascivious thoughts that made the lips between my legs swell and pucker. I smiled. Now I understood why people lived small, circumscribed lives. It was easier. Weeks ago, when my sexuality had been repressed, I had felt fine. But now that I was more alive, I had to deal with it. How? I felt all dressed up with nowhere to go.

Stop thinking about him. He's not even interested in you. Not like that.

I sighed. It was true. Harley had made his lack of interest perfectly clear the night we went swimming. Like a logical parent, my mind rehashed all the arguments why I shouldn't think about him, but my body wouldn't listen. My body wanted him. Wanted him as I had not wanted a man before. Not even Bart.

Meanwhile, I looked over the two dozen plants I'd bought: tomato plants, zucchini, green pepper, lettuce and a few broccoli and cauliflowers. They all looked tremblingly tiny. That these fragile little things were strong enough to hold the virile forces of spring was truly amazing.

I looked up and saw Elfy coming across the yard, her ginger hair zigzagging out from under a new Toronto Blue Jays cap.

Kneeling down, she emptied a canvas bag of stones into my hands. "A present. From Lake Superior. I got them the last time I was there and thought we might make a sort of cairn of them somewhere. For good luck."

I moved my hand over the smooth, cool surfaces of the stones. I could almost feel the waves sliding along them, licking them round and slippery.

"Agatha would think we've gone dotty, but never mind." Elfy set the stones aside. "This where you're going to put the garden?" She surveyed the area in front of us. "Looks good to me. Got a rototiller?"

I shook my head. "My neighbour, Mr. Grimes, does, but I doubt if he'll lend it. He's persnickety about stuff like that."

"Be best if we got one. We want the soil light. Fluffy as angel cake. So the bugs can move around and do their thing." She disappeared across the yard and in a few minutes, came back pushing the machine across the lawn, grinning. "I taught him everything he knows about begonias."

"You did? Your list of accomplishments is endless."

Elfy shook her head. "I've just been around so long it looks good." She eyed me knowingly.

"How's it going?" I didn't want to ask, but ever since that night with the champagne I'd been worried.

"Hell on wheels some days. It helps to keep busy. And I'm not making myself any fancy promises. One hour at a time. That's all I can handle." Throwing her shoulders back, she said, "Come on, I'll show you how to use this thing." She pulled the starter cord and began to push the machine through the soil, leaving a trail of fresh, moist earth behind her.

After awhile, I took my turn and was surprised how hard it was. "It's like pushing a baby carriage through the mud."

"With twins in it," Elfy said. "But don't make it look too hard or your neighbour will be over here trying to do it for us. I had to talk him out of pushing it over here as it was. He's one of those people who thinks old people can't do things!" She sighed and turned to the seedlings. Later, she led me around the garden while we discussed the best location for each type of plant.

"Once," she said, touching the foliage of a zucchini leaf, "once I planted a whole garden when I was in a snit about something. Not a blessed thing came up." She smiled self-consciously. "I'd know better now." Adroitly, she positioned the plants where they were going to be dug in. Then she gathered her things. "You can handle it from here, can't you? The biggest part's done and I told Agatha I'd help with the Gzowski interview."

"Peter Gzowski? Of Morningside?"

"Didn't I tell you?" Elfy blushed and grinned at the same time. "I forget who I've told what to, so much has been happening. Gzowski wants a telephone interview. He wanted two Grannies. I was going to ask you, but I knew Agatha's knickers would get in a knot and we'd never hear the end of it."

"Well, well . . . you did the right thing. Do a good one!"

As she left, she kissed my cheek quickly. The kiss felt strong and slightly wet, reminding me of the way my sister used to kiss me when I was little.

"What's that for?" I asked, feeling warm in my chest.

"I don't know. I guess you're starting to feel like family. Scary as that is."

I put my arm around her tenderly. Given the amount of pain Elfy had suffered from her previous family, I could understand why the feeling was frightening. It was a bit frightening how special Elfy was becoming to me as well.

"Maybe we can make a new type of family," I said. "Instead of being tied by blood, we'll be joined by spirit."

"A kindred spirits club. I like it. But don't tell Aggie. She'd want to join and be president." She laughed, waved and was off.

After Elfy left, I played in the garden like a kid, taking off my shoes and letting the earth squish up between my toes. I organized the plants, then slowly began digging them in, pressing them firmly into the soil and watering each one from a new watering can.

It amazed me how each plant had such a distinct feeling to it. The zucchini and squash plants had a "ready-set-GO!" energy. They were spreading their leaves, eager to take over the entire garden. The blue-green broccoli plants felt bold and substantial. The milky-green cauliflowers were gentler, but sturdy nonetheless.

Warm from the work, I stripped down to my tee-shirt. The sun caressed my skin, waking my senses. When I had half of the seedlings planted, I sat and watered the whole garden, happily squashing my thumb over the end of the hose to make the spray gentle and light. The soil became dark, sucking up the water like a thirst-starved infant. Feeling hot now, I held the hose over my head until my insides ran cold.

Crazy old lady. I smiled. Why would any woman not want to get old? Getting old gave us freedom. Freedom to do what we never would have done otherwise. I stripped off my wet clothes and lay in a secluded spot to dry. Oh, the loveliness of sun and skin together. Ozone or not, this was a love affair I was going to indulge in. The heat lay heavily upon me and my body felt plump with the pleasure of it.

Nature has always been sensual to me. As a teenager, with provocations in my body I didn't understand, I'd often wandered deep in the woods. It was safe there. In the woods I could let these feelings be. The woods seemed to understand.

One early spring day, I'd come upon an enchanted little glade of greenery, secretly tucked away behind some lavishly-leafed shrubs and rocks covered with lichen. Everything was still wet in this hidden place, with pools of black and silver water puddling on the ground. The moss there was moist and spongy to my touch. As I stood, a shaft of sunlight penetrated the lushness and a surge of energy shot through me. Enlivened, my body became a being with its own demands. The first was a feverish compulsion to be naked. Feeling protected in the womb of this little grove, I took off my clothes.

I wandered over to a fallen tree trunk, thickly covered with a mass of emerald green moss. I straddled it, and as the coolness of the moss met the lips between my legs, pleasure erupted throughout my body. For a moment I lay down on the massive trunk and hugged it. But my body's ripeness demanded more and I found myself gently sliding my breasts along the moss. Exquisite sensations rippled through me. Feeling hot and thick, I sat up and spread my legs further to embrace the furry hardness of the wet log. I arched back with the intensity of the enjoyment and gripped the bark of the tree as I moved rhythmically against it. A light rain began to trickle down my chest, cold on my nipples.

Sensations torpedoed through me, each adding to a burgeoning pressure for something to happen. My body became one steadfast demand that some animal part of me seemed to know about, seemed willing to gallop towards, moving my thighs and hips in new ways. Out of control now, I cantered from pleasure to pleasure until my body suddenly reared up in an enraptured burst of feeling.

Stunned, I fell against the tree trunk, my heart pounding. What had happened? Wondering if such an act might cause paralysis or something, I moved a bit to make sure I still could and was relieved to feel my body responding as usual. I waited until my breath returned to normal. Surely, there would be some punishment for this. Would I get warts? Or a rash? Or get pregnant?

Dazed, I dressed and went home. For weeks, I wondered what had happened. Surprisingly, life went forward, carrying this amazing experience in its stride. Did this happen to other people? If it did, how did it ever stay so secret? It was like trying to hide fireworks.

My body, however, continued to make its demands and I soon found ways of experiencing these inner explosions even in my bed at home. It was incredible to me that my body could feel such an immensity of pleasure through my own touch.

With such remembrances floating through my mind
and the warm sun on my body, I fell into a deep sleep
beside my newly planted garden. I dreamt of riding a
horse bareback through an enchanted forest. Then the
horse turned into Harley and I woke up.

Feeling exceedingly thirsty, I pulled on a shirt and
walked with the rest of my clothes back to the house. As I
moved, my body felt robust and full. Like a blossoming
rhododendron, round, resplendent and ripe. Harley,
where are you?

Inside the house, the phone rang. I tensed. There was
something disturbing about the way it rang. I listened to
my answering machine encouraging the caller to leave a
message. Sometimes I turned the sound down so I
wouldn't hear the person's voice leaving the message. That
gave me the option of staying tuned out. Once I listened,
I knew I was putting myself at risk. Some calls, if heard,
could not be ignored. Over the years I'd learned to
differentiate with remarkable precision which calls had to
be responded to and when. From the sound of Norman's
voice, there was no option about replying. Besides, he
wasn't giving me one. He was on his way over, taking a
chance that I might be around. If I weren't, he planned to
wait in his car until I was. So his message said. An
impulsive act for a man like Norman.

I shivered and hopped into the shower. When his car
pulled up, I was dressed and ready. I had the candle
burning when he entered my office.

Norman walked unsteadily to my office, then slumped
in the chair without speaking. I couldn't see directly into
his eyes because he kept them away from me.

I understood why he didn't talk. Rarely could words

wrap themselves around the kind of intensity he was obviously experiencing. He needed time to find his way and I was willing to give it to him.

"It's not fair," he finally said. Not wanting to distract in any way from his process, I kept quiet.

"All my life I've worked hard," he began. "Played by the rules. Ha! The rules." His tongue moved in his mouth as if trying to cleanse it of an awful taste. "My mother was big on rules. If you knew the rules and stuck by them, everything was supposed to be all right. What a fucking lie that turned out to be."

Silently, he shook his head, incredulous at the injustice. As if reporting to a judge, he went over his good behaviour. "I've done all the right things. Worked in the right companies. Joined the right clubs. Hung around with the right people. I'm supposed to have it made." His eyes widened as they stared at the carpet.

He was quiet again. While he gathered himself to say more, I thought about the belief so many people have that if they do the right things, their good behaviour will protect them from the bad things in life. Obviously Norman had realized the delusion. But what had happened?

"It's like I was in a trance," he continued, "and now I've woken up." He sat without moving for several minutes.

His eyes now jumped to mine and held on for dear life. "The cancer is back." He dug his curled fingers into the arms of the chair.

I swallowed. Took a breath. Tried to reestablish my equilibrium. I felt dizzy, nauseated. Breathe, breathe, I told myself.

"The doctors aren't very hopeful." He sighed heavily. "I can either die quickly with a gun. Or slowly with chemotherapy. Or hope there is a God and I'll be spared."

"Can they operate?"

"My chances are better with the chemo. So the doctor says." He paused. "They're holding a room for me at the Cancer Clinic right now. Every minute I wait increases the cancer's chance of getting me."

I looked over at Norman. He sat collapsed in his chair like a condemned man. I waited for him to speak.

"Why now? Why now?"

"Yes, why now?" I repeated his words, still feeling shaky.

Norman looked down, fighting emotion.

"What if it were possible to put the cancer over there in that empty chair," I suggested, grappling for some way of dealing with this. I watched Norman's eyes dart cautiously to the chair and saw him seeing things. "What would the cancer say if it could talk?"

"It would say, 'I'm trying to kill you,'" Norman answered, his voice twisted with sarcasm.

"But why? Why is it trying to kill you? What would it say if you asked it?"

Norman shrugged, deciding to go with my lead. "It's saying, 'Live! Live!' As stupid as that sounds."

"Why stupid?"

"Because it's telling me to live, but meanwhile, it's killing me."

"How would it have you live? What would it make different?"

The words tumbled out, surprising us both. "I'd have to quit my job. Travel. Ski. Do all the things I wanted to do as a kid and couldn't. All the things I still can't do."

"Still can't?"

"Well, I could, if I wanted to throw away everything I've ever worked for." He stopped, thinking about his words. "Throw away or have taken away . . ." Using his sleeve, he wiped a tear from the corner of his eye.

I held the box of tissues towards him, but he shook his head. "What does your cancer think of chemotherapy?"

Norman was thoughtful for a moment. "It's not worried. It can beat any chemo, it says." He paused, listening to himself. "What it would have a harder time beating is me being happy."

"What would make you happy, Norman?"

"Skiing." He smiled for the first time. "But, Jesus, I can't just quit everything and throw a knapsack on my back."

I looked at him without speaking.

"Can I?" Norman asked. Asking the question seemed to open some inner window of possibility, and for the first time, I saw some light cross his haggard face.

"Your life is yours, Norman," I said quietly. "To live in whatever way you feel is right for you."

"What should I do?"

"I have no idea. But what I do know is that from what you've told me, you've lived a lot of your life meeting other people's expectations. Perhaps this illness is giving you a chance to find out just what you want."

Norman was pensive. I noticed he was no longer staring at the carpet but had turned into himself, deeply attending to his own inner process. I was glad. I knew that was the beginning place.

"I've got a lot to think about." He looked at me now, tired, as if he'd just hauled himself out of a raging sea to a beach. He stood up and I hugged him. For the first time ever, I felt my hug go into him.

"Watch your dreams," I whispered at the door, wishing I had something more profound to say. I felt helpless, sad and inadequate.

Norman turned and left. As the door closed, I felt darkness descend.

Chapter 12

After Norman left, I paced the living room, glancing out the window at the little plants still waiting to be dug into the soil. There was little chance of that now. Knowing I could do no more in the garden, I pulled out an old sleeping bag and lay on a deck chair on the back porch.

It wasn't fair that Norman was dying. He had so much living to do. That was the hard part, that he was being ripped away from life before he was finished. It made me feel panicky. As if there were no time to lose.

Once I'd read about a tribe of aborigines in Australia where people only died when they had determined that their time had come. According to the story, when the person was ready to go, they said goodbye to their families and went alone into the desert. There, they shut their bodily processes down until they were no longer alive.

That's the way it should be. Death should be a friend at the end of the road, not an enemy.

I thought about my own medical tests, the ones I'd had redone yesterday. What would I do if the doctor came back with a diagnosis like Norman's? I'd be furious. Not because I had to die, but because I hadn't yet lived.

I'd spent so much time analyzing my life and everyone else's, I'd somehow missed fully living it. For years, I'd functioned and functioned well. But wasn't there more to life than functioning? What about passion, what about ecstasy, what about inner peace? If I died, would anyone really care? Would the world be even slightly better because of my life? Was there one person I had gone to the depth and breadth of my heart with?

I stared mournfully at the lake. The day dimmed and cooled and I pulled the sleeping bag more firmly around me. Dozing off, I dreamt I was in a grey forest looking for Harley, but I couldn't find him. When I woke up, a maelstrom of stars stretched out above me. Unimaginably wild. Yet the darkness between the stars was so black and threatening, I could hardly look at it.

I kept picturing my doctor telling me I had cancer. I imagined myself having radiation, then chemotherapy, then felt the surgeon's knife cut away my cancerous breast. Fear tightened around me like a wire.

Oh, Rudi, I need you. I conjured up the woman's hawk-like eyes. Eyes that saw everything as if from a great height.

Life is too hard.

I could almost hear her answer. "Yes, it's hard. Scary too, but only sometimes. Are you going to give up living it because of that? What about helping yourself through the scary times? You can't change them, but you can change how you respond to them."

Sounds like a lot of work, I wanted to answer back. I was sick of working my life, analyzing my patterns. What I wanted was someone to arrive at my door and nourish me. Hey, you there, God, if you exist, bring that to me. Bring Harley.

After a while I got up and made myself a cup of hot milk and took it back outside. That settled me and I was able to look at the situation a little differently. What if on some deep, unconscious level, Norman had created this crisis to push him into making a shift? I knew from my years of psychotherapeutic work how difficult it was for people to change tracks. Even when that change was necessary for their survival. Sometimes they needed a jump start.

Norman had a lot vested in the life he was living. Kids, private schools, country clubs, social position. If, as I suspected, Norman was not living in tune with his true self, his psyche had been faced with the daunting job of needing to dismantle his life structure and replace it with a more relevant one. Could the shock of this news and the fear it engendered be powerful enough to wrench him out of the old routines and into a new direction?

I thought about other clients whose bodily conditions had woken them up. Janice's ulcers, for example, had forced her to stand up for her needs. Allan's hearing problems had made him confront his father's verbal abuse. And Lyle. Thinking about Lyle made me smile.

Lyle was the kind of man who smelled of Ivory soap. The kind who would do a good deed for anyone. The kind who showed up at my door, guts twisted in a knot after he'd lied to his wife and spent the night having reckless sex with someone he'd just met.

It was always the same with a man like that. After he had realized I wasn't interested in playing God and judging his behaviour, he'd relaxed enough to let me help him understand himself. What I found when I talked with Lyle was a history of repression. The waitress wasn't the problem, she was the result of the problem. And the problem was that Lyle had to wake up to his need to live more fully. If he listened to himself, he could find ways to do that legitimately. If he didn't listen, his body would find whatever cheap thrills it could. His soul was hungry. It was insisting on being fed. How he fed it was his only choice.

I was always awed, watching a person's life force at work. It was incredible the way it could be held back for a while or diverted, sometimes even tricked into thinking it was getting what it needed, but in the end, it called the shots. Like a seedling, it could look fragile, but break up a slab of concrete in its effort to live itself out. Was this what Norman's illness was all about, a ferocious shakeup to get him living more authentically? I lay for a long while thinking about it.

Light was just beginning to inhale itself into the day when Harley appeared. I felt him before I saw him, felt the force of his body beside me.

"You're here." A warm pleasure moved through me. I drew him close, feeling the steady beat of his heart.

"I was thinking about you all day yesterday," he said softly. "But I was in Wawa and it took me a while to get back. Is everything all right?"

Up close like this, I could feel the vibration of his voice in his body. I tried to speak, but my throat thickened. His appearance confused and overwhelmed me. How had he known to come? And what did it mean?

"Having a bad time?"

"Bad today," I said, forcing the words out. "A client just found out he has cancer." I wished I could add the rest of it: *And it's brought up all my own fears about dying.*

Harley looked at me a long moment as if he'd heard the words I had not said. He surveyed the yard. "Come on," he said, taking my hand. "Big troubles need big solutions." Gently, but firmly he eased me up and led me down into the garden where Elfy and I had rototilled yesterday. My bare feet tingled as I walked through the cool, early morning dew.

Clearing a space over the loamy soil, he picked up the shovel and dug a small trench.

"Now, lie down."

"In there?" I took a step back. It looked like a pit for a coffin.

"Yep." His wide face was soft with amusement. "Just for a while. Trust me."

"Clothes and all?"

"It's just earth. Not ink." A smile slipped over his full lips. "You can take your clothes off if you want. I won't mind."

I lay down with my clothes on. Immediately, I felt the cool support of the earth. As if it could take the weight of all the troubles in the world and still hold me up. I let myself sink down into it.

I was just beginning to relax when I realized Harley was heaping soil over my ankles and up my legs. Startled, I lifted my head.

"It's all right. I'm just going to put a covering of earth over your body. You'll still be able to move and breathe. Honest." He broke into a wide smile. "Honest Injun." Chuckling to himself, he carried on mounding the moist earth over me.

Slivers of apprehension wheedled through me. Yet as his hands smoothed the cool soil over my legs, I found the weight and feel of it solid and comforting. I began to relax. When he packed the soil around my hips and pelvis, wondrous feelings of sexual aliveness brawled through my body.

He piled a thick mound of earth on the centre of my chest, between my breasts. The weight of the earth there felt like a hand. It was as if the earth were extending a great paw of understanding for all the pain I'd suffered. Tears broke from my eyes.

Keeping one comforting hand on my shoulder, Harley continued to gather soil around my neck and head, leaving most of my face uncovered. Then he moved so that he was sitting near my head.

"I'll stay with you."

I could hardly hear him, the pull of the earth was so strong. Like a great mother, it wrapped me in its embrace and I felt a huge relief as I sank into it. Down and down I went into the still cradle of its peace. Time passed. Once, I opened my eyes and saw the boughs of several trees arching above me. Another time I heard a robin chirping and felt a light hopping over my thigh. Hours passed.

Sometime much later, I felt myself grin. "This is wonderful."

"Makes you understand why flowers flower," Harley said. "They get to keep their feet in this stuff all the time." He thought for a while, then added. "I learned about it from Felix. A crazy dog of his got skunked once and he buried it like this. The earth took the smell away. Took his craziness too. So I tried it." Pleasure moved across his face. "Now I'm only half crazy."

I heard a deep chuckling sound come from my chest.

"Time to come out, I think," Harley said. "When you start laughing, it's a sure sign you're done."

I felt sad. "I'm not sure I want to come out."

"Feels good, doesn't it?" Harley smiled. "Remember this when you think of your friend dying. His body will come home to this." He looked at me tenderly. "His body will be in the arms of mother earth. And his spirit will be in the sky, flying like a bird. But the sky part is another lesson. We'll save that for another day."

I closed my eyes, savouring the last few minutes of the huge earth hug I was wrapped in. If this is death, there is nothing to be afraid of. I knew that now.

"Come on out," Harley said. "Before you start sprouting leaves."

Reluctantly, I began to move my legs and arms, until finally I was out of the soil and standing up. "I feel like a chick, fresh out of the egg." I looked down at myself. Smears of earth covered my clothes and body. Granules of earth fell from my hair as I moved, but I felt wonderful.

"Time for the lake," Harley said and we walked together to the dock.

Normally, I liked to dive in, but today I edged myself into the lake, leaving my clothes on so the water could wash away the soil. As I stood, water up to my knees, I looked up and saw Harley taking his clothes off. He wasn't sinewy and lean like Bart had been, but I liked that. Bart's body had never offered much solace. Harley's body, however, had a firm roundness to it, looked strong yet comforting, as if it could receive as well as give. His thighs were long muscular curves of tanned skin.

This isn't fair, I thought. I must look as mucky as a worm, and he's standing there naked and beautiful. Harley dove into the lake and ended my misery.

I swam quickly, then walked up to the house,

muttering to myself. *What does this man think, that I'm too old to be turned on by a man's body?*

By the time Harley had finished swimming, I had changed my clothes and made breakfast.

"Great," Harley said, seeing the large tray of breakfast things. He looked at me with inquisitive eyes, trying to read my mood.

We took the tray outside and sat under the apple tree. I chose to sit there because from the house it looked so lovely with its delicate pinkish-white blossoms. But now I found the voluptuous apple blossoms overpowering. I felt like I was standing next to a big-breasted woman on a packed, swaying bus. The sensual abundance was so unavoidable, so unapologetic, so loose, that it suddenly seemed ridiculous that Harley and I were sitting eating breakfast when all I wanted to do was take off my clothes and lie with him.

My body was leaning towards him and I pulled it back. *Don't throw yourself at him. He isn't interested.*

I busied myself making tea. Our fingers met over the honey spoon. He grunted and let me use the spoon first. Quietly, he sat back against the tree.

"Feels like a storm." He squinted into the horizon.

I nodded. Yes. The air felt heavy as if gathering itself for something. Silently, I drank my tea and watched. Suddenly the temperature dropped and the birds stopped singing. I found myself holding my breath in anticipation.

Like a drum beat, the storm was upon us. Big, juicy drops splashed on the ground. Under the tree we had some protection but the apple blossoms let fly, tossing themselves into the wind, shamelessly splaying their pink, floppy bodies over everything.

Harley's whole being seemed to be absorbed in the storm. He pulled me to my feet and ran with me headlong into the wind. We raced across the field, the rain thundering down around us. As if to capture the full force of it, Harley dropped my hand and yanked off his shirt. He pulled off his hair tie so the black rope of it swung free and fanned out wildly in the wind. Arching back, he reached his arms out, his palms up and the rain pounded on his bare skin. Then he made a loud whooping sound that made the hair on my skin go erect.

"YEEEOOOOOOOO. . ."

I closed my eyes and listened as he made the sound over and over, letting it lead me back to some primordial, instinctual place where only sound could enter. Beside him, I could feel the drumming of his feet on the wet grasses as his body moved in a rhythmic rain dance his body knew and understood.

He was beside me now, his wet face shining, his voice hoarse. "Make your sound . . ."

"My sound? I don't know how . . ."

"Trust yourself."

I closed my eyes nervously, madly trying to figure out what I was supposed to do. A loud bang of thunder jolted me, took my attention down to my feet and the earth. Thoughts dropped away and a force came up from the ground, vibrated in my throat and flew out my lungs.

It was an ecstatic sound, the kind a child might make as it leapt into water or rolled in the first snow, a delighted, rapturous whoop. It was so joyful, I let it happen again, offering it to the heavens as I thrust my head back and let go.

Wonderment bloomed on Harley's face. He took my

hands. Lightning flashed and we stood looking at each other with open, seeing eyes. Although he reached his hand towards me gently and I saw the caress coming, it seemed to take forever to reach me and I felt as if I had been waiting for eons and even then, when his hand did touch my face, my body jolted and for a moment, I wondered if I'd been struck by lightning.

He touched my hair, my throat, my chest, stroking and stroking as I stood with my eyes closed. I became a delirium of responses exquisitely sharp and pleasurable. His touches streaked through me like wind in the grasses, tossing sensations everywhere. His hand moved over my belly, down my thighs and then, for a moment, rested on my vulva, as if in greeting. Slowly Harley bent down and planted a soft kiss where his hand had been. It was such a cherishing act, tears came to my eyes.

We lay down on a thick patch of moss near the lake. Now he let me draw him close and I felt a deep homecoming as our naked bodies touched. For the rest of the morning, I experienced what it was like to be a wild thing, considered sacred, yet greatly desired.

Chapter 13

Harley stayed late into the day. Shamelessly, we talked, laughed and made love outside, as if we lived a hundred miles from civilization. Every once in a while a thought pierced the aura of my bliss. *What if someone sees us?* Or: *Aren't I too OLD for this sort of thing?* Like arrows shot into a river, these thoughts were soon lost in the frothy swirl of sensuality that was streaming through me. All I was aware of was the feeling of sun on my back, the wind on my tummy and Harley, Harley, Harley.

I feasted on him. Knowing that all too soon life's normal routines were going to recapture me, I gorged myself on the wild fruit of him, body and soul. When it was time for Harley to leave, we had to untangle ourselves from each other, limb by limb.

"I don't know when I'll be back," he said. He took the eagle feather from his hat and put it in my hair. "I have to go away on band business again. Then there's a conference . . ."

I became quiet, realizing all the more deeply that Harley had a life in the native world that I wasn't a part of. I wondered if it bothered him that I was white. Did he feel he was betraying something by being with me?

As if reading my thoughts, he pointed to my heart. "What colour are you in there?" he tapped my chest. "Same as me, I think. Same as me." He wrapped his big, bear-like body around me in one last appreciative hug and was gone.

I put the feather in the hat he'd given me and sat under a tree, enjoying the sweet feelings in my body. It was late afternoon and a lovely dappled light was coming through the trees into the yard. Everything smelled clean and fresh and looked plump from the morning storm. There was a satisfied, contented feeling in the air, and I didn't want to go in.

After sitting for a while, I let Charlie out and began rearranging the plants Harley had moved aside to make room for my earth bed. I smoothed over the soil with a rake, put the plants back into position, then began digging them in.

"I've warmed it up for you," I told them, as I put them into the earth.

I was just finishing when Elfy appeared, a devilish smile playing at her mouth. "Took you a long time to get those plants in, eh?"

Feeling giddy and self-conscious, I kept my focus on the garden. Elfy was acting as if she knew something. How could she?

Elfy nodded with amused understanding. "Well, whatever the distraction was, it looks good on you. Like someone's loosened your strings." She broke into a convulsive chuckle.

Not wanting to look at Elfy in case I'd blush, I lifted one of the last plants out of its pot, eased it into a hole and gently tucked the soil around it.

"Amazing how good those Indian feathers can make you feel," Elfy carried on with mock seriousness.

I reached up and touched the feather in my hat. I'd forgotten I was wearing it.

"That mean you're going steady?"

I couldn't stop the blush. It flushed up into my face and made my ears burn.

"Oh, go on." Elfy grinned, "don't get all shy about it. I'm glad you enjoyed yourself. I just wish I'd bumped into the two of you instead of Robyn."

"Robyn?" The blood drained from my face.

Elfy studied me jovially. "What are you so embarrassed about? All Robyn said was that you had a man visiting." She shook her head. "Youth is so wasted on the young."

"What time was this?"

"About two hours ago. She's at my house now, watching television. I asked her to have dinner with me."

I nodded absently while trying to figure out what Robyn might have seen. If she'd seen us two hours ago, Harley and I should have at least had our clothes on. I cringed with embarrassment.

"Goodness, glory be! Relax! It's not as if she caught the two of you running around naked. Although you're acting as if she did, so it must have been a close call. But all she said to me was that she saw you kiss the man and walk him to his car."

Elfy tipped the last plant out of its pot with her small, blue-veined hands. I took it, avoiding her eyes. I felt like a child caught with a candy in her mouth.

"Robyn has to grow up sometime," Elfy carried on blithely. "I remember catching my parents in, how shall I put it – in a state of disarray? On the sunporch. I grew up that day. At least, it felt like I did. My mother was never apologetic. Even after my father died, she had a lover. She was seventy-five then." Elfy sighed. "Never knew why people think sex dries up with age. That's like thinking a bottle of wine dries up instead of getting more mellow."

"Ever think you might get together with someone?" I asked, trying to shift the focus on to her. I began gathering up the garden tools.

"Maybe." Elfy was more serious now. "You never can tell, can you, about life. When something's going to be given to us." She frowned. "Or taken away."

"Should I phone Robyn, do you think?"

Elfy made an impatient, dismissive gesture with her hand. "She's still adjusting to all the changes, that's all. But as I told her, these days, if you're living, you're changing. There's no two ways about it." Elfy picked up a rake and followed me to the garden shed.

"How did the interview go with Gzowski?"

She grinned. "Couldn't get a word in edgewise. But Aggie made everything sound so good, I didn't mind. She even mentioned the new tree calendar. So we should sell even more. We might have to print another batch. They're going like hot cakes."

"Good. Now we'll have some money for the community meeting."

"Yeah, it'll pay for that hot shot speaker from Earth Ecology. Even if he speaks for free, it would be good to offer him something for his time. We can do that now, thanks to Robyn's calendars."

Pride surged through me.

"Did you know, Estelle's still trying to dig up some dirt about Boyd," Elfy said, chatting on. "If anyone can do it, she can. She should have been a Mountie, that woman. Old people would make great undercover agents. People say anything to old people. Because they think old people don't count. Don't you think Estelle would make a good undercover cop? She's so distinguished looking, no one would ever guess. Her eyes are bad, but – "

"What is the matter with Estelle's eyes?" I asked. "I've never been able to figure out why they bulge so much."

Elfy grimaced. "I've never heard it from her, but a cousin of hers once told me that Estelle's parents used to lock her in a cupboard when they went out. So she wouldn't get into trouble when they were away. Once they left her in there for most of a day and when they came back, her eyes were like that."

Both of us were quiet. "I guess that was back in the days when people could do whatever they wanted with children," Elfy said.

"I have clients who still think they can do whatever they want with children," I commented.

"How's your speech coming?" Elfy asked.

"My speech? No ideas yet . . ."

"Better get it ready. I've invited a whole bunch of Earth Elders. They're going to want to hear something pretty good."

"Earth Elders? Who are they?" I picked up the hose and began watering the plants.

"I talked to you about it, didn't I? I thought I did." She shook her head and laughed. "Too much for my brain to remember who I've told what to. Anyway, you know how we've been getting letters from people asking if they can help? Well, I thought we should give them a chance to get involved. Not just with our issue, although that would be all right too, but with other ecology things. Before I knew it, I'd organized an Earth Elder's Festival."

"When's it going to be?"

"It starts the day of the community meeting."

"Elfy! Isn't that loading things up?"

"I thought it would help having more people around to support us. Besides, another woman, Ruth, is arranging most of it." Elfy took a big breath and looked at me sheepishly. "All kinds of people want to come."

I changed topics. "What's the update on Boyd and Abernathy?" Abernathy was one of the town councillors that the Grannies thought was on the take from Boyd.

"Joey's still convinced there's hanky-panky. Abernathy always votes in favour of any development Boyd's involved in and he lives high off the hog for a guy on a councillor's salary. But Boyd is smooth. He's going to cover his tracks."

"Yes, but his overconfidence is bound to trip him up sometimes."

"More sooner than later, we hope," Elfy said as she watched the slow, rhythmic swaying of the hose. Then she turned and looked over across the field. "Here, Charlie," she called. She waited a moment, then turned to me anxiously. "What's the matter with the dog? He hurt his foot or something?"

I looked up to see Charlie limping through the grass. Then I realized he was not just limping but veering unsteadily from side to side. He stopped, retched forcefully and tried to walk, but buckled over.

"Charlie!" I threw down the hose and ran to him. When I reached him, he lay with his eyes closed. He was barely breathing. Whatever it was, it was serious. I looked at Elfy desperately.

"I've got to get him to the vet. Can you get my car keys? They're – " I gesticulated wildly. "The peg by the door."

Weak-kneed and frightened, I managed to half carry, half drag Charlie to the car where Elfy helped lift him inside.

"You sit with him," Elfy said. "I'll drive."

Elfy drove like a wild woman, turning corners so fast the tires screeched. Even from the back seat, I heard the old woman's breath coming in short gasps.

When we reached the animal hospital, the nurse, seeing the anguish on my face, led us quickly into one of the examining rooms and called the doctor. The vet raised Charlie's eyelids, took his pulse and immediately gave him an injection.

"Looks like poison."

"Poison!" Elfy repeated, her voice booming.

I put my hand on Elfy's arm to steady myself.

The doctor adjusted his chrome-rimmed glasses. "Might be wolf bait. I know some farmers who've lost sheep lately. Sometimes they leave poison out to bait the wolves."

My mind raced to thoughts of the local farmers. Would any of them do such a thing? They knew I had a dog.

"Or maybe he got into some rat poison. He's eaten a good dose of it, whatever it was."

"Is he going to be all right?" My chest was tight and it was hard to speak.

The vet's brow furrowed. "I don't know. We'll have to wait and see."

Outside, I sucked in air. I had to think and yet I couldn't think. I got in the car and Elfy, looking white as tissue paper, crawled in beside me.

"I don't like this." I steadied my hands enough to put the key in the ignition. "I don't like this one bit."

"You know who did it, don't you?"

I looked at her. "No . . ." She said the word as soon as it formed in my mind.

"Boyd!"

My head ached. Could even Boyd do such a thing? A roll of anger swelled through me. I couldn't deal with this right now. It was hard enough coping with Charlie being sick. I was about to speak, but one look at Elfy's sagging, discouraged face and I decided not to. Silently, I drove her home.

When we reached her house, I parked and turned to her. Her eyes looked as dead as tree stumps in a swamp.

"Do you still want Robyn to stay for dinner?" I asked. "The company might do you good." Seeing Elfy nod, I reached over and squeezed her arm affectionately. I was glad Elfy was keeping Robyn with her. I didn't want Elfy to be alone. Not in the shape she was in. "Send her back in the morning if you like. But meanwhile, take care of yourself, will you?" I looked at Elfy with deep concern. She seemed to be crumpling before my very eyes.

Back at home, I lay out on the grass near where I'd been covered in earth that morning. Again, I felt the comfort of the soil as it met my body. Worried thoughts kept breaking into my mind, but the trees and soil seemed to draw them away. Soon, I fell into a deep sleep. When I awoke, it was cold and dark. Slowly I pulled myself up and went into the house.

Chapter 14

First thing the next morning, I called the vet. Charlie was still holding on. I phoned Elfy to tell her the good news, but there was no answer.

In a few minutes, I heard Robyn downstairs. Maybe Elfy was out because she had been driving Robyn home. But then why hadn't Elfy come in? I called down to ask Robyn if she wanted to join me for a cup of tea. I was going to have to face her sometime and buoyed by the good news about Charlie, I decided it might as well be now.

Robyn wandered into the living room and perched herself on the armchair, looking ready to fly off at any time. Although her skin was pale and white, there were shadows of darkness just beneath the surface.

"Maybe we should talk," I said.

"There's nothing to talk about, mother."

My arms tingled. I wanted to shake her. Shake her or hold her, anything to make contact. I sighed and decided to go more slowly. "Is Elfy all right this morning?"

"Fine," Robyn said in a soft, insouciant voice.

Right. Robyn was so self-absorbed, she probably didn't even notice Elfy's low mood. She hadn't even asked about Charlie.

"Elfreda's weird," Robyn said, looking out the window.

"What do you mean, weird?"

Robyn grimaced. "Going on about Charlie being poisoned. Crazy stuff like that."

I stiffened. "He was poisoned."

"Maybe, but no one did it . . ."

Anger sputtered inside me. "We don't know that."

Robyn's eyes glared. "You're being paranoid."

My body took the hit, but I carried on, trying to explain. "I know that some people in this town are angry about the tree campaign. They think saving the trees means jobs are going to be lost. I wouldn't put it past some of them to try and get back at us. I certainly wouldn't put it past someone like Boyd."

Robyn's eyes flew open. "Boyd?"

"Boyd!" I repeated, holding my ground.

"I don't know why you don't watch Charlie more if you care for him like you say you do. Tie him up."

"What do you mean, 'like I say I do'? Charlie's never been tied in his life! He'd hate it."

Heat surged down my arms. I wanted to hit Robyn and hit her hard. I, who had never even spanked Robyn as a child, now burned with the desire to slap some sense into her. But what was the use? I couldn't beat Robyn into waking up. Tiredness swept over me. I felt as though I were being punished. But for what? For my afternoon with Harley? Maybe that was part of it, but this felt older than that.

The phone rang. Robyn and I stared at each other, neither moving. "Can't make our walk this morning," Madge said to the machine. "Catch you later, alligator." There was the sound of a giggle and then a dial tone.

I moved towards the phone. I knew I'd get Madge's

machine, knew Madge's current location as surely as I knew the spot where the raccoon got into the garbage bin. Even though I knew she wasn't home, I could leave a message. "Tell your bastard of a boyfriend, better luck next time – Charlie's still alive." I picked up the phone to do just that, then put it down again. Yelling into someone's answering machine was going a little far, even for me.

I turned back to Robyn. "Look, I can't say that Boyd was the one who poisoned Charlie, but I do know that if Boyd didn't do it, he could have. Boyd is a man with no scruples. As far as I'm concerned, anyone who could fell hundred-year-old trees could also poison a dog." I looked at Robyn. There was an unoccupied look in her eyes. "But I guess you can't see that," I said aloud, more to myself than to Robyn, who was beyond my grasp now. I shook my head. Why was she insisting on being so blind?

The phone rang again. This time I answered it.

"Agatha here, Jess. Just heard the news about Charlie. Is there anything I can do?"

"No, but thanks . . ." Despite Agatha's confident manner, there was an uneasiness in her voice.

"Is the prognosis good?"

"It's not bad, let's put it that way."

"Do you think it was an accident?"

I shrugged, watching Robyn slip away. Why was it that the two of us couldn't be in the same room for more than two minutes without arguing?

"I have no idea what to think," I said to Agatha, my voice sounding defeated.

"Why don't you call the police? It wouldn't hurt to keep Boyd on his toes with a few questions from the authorities."

"I suppose." I was feeling more tired by the minute.

"Meanwhile, what are we going to do about Elfreda?" Agatha asked.

"What do you mean?" I sighed. I didn't want to talk anymore.

"I've just spoken with her and she sounded – off."

I didn't want to hear this. "She's in shock, that's all. When we found Charlie, it took a lot out of her. She's really fond of him. Remember, she has no resilience yet and things knock her around sometimes. She's still in recovery."

"Recovery! That slur in her voice didn't sound like recovery!"

"No." The word didn't make it out of my mouth.

"It doesn't take much to detect a slur," Agatha said, slighted.

I felt myself sinking. All I wanted was to climb into bed and pull the covers over my head.

"We need to have a meeting."

"Probably," I said halfheartedly. "Maybe in a few days." I wanted to give Elfy time to recuperate. The woman was probably just tuckered out. Tiredness could make a person's voice sound slurry, couldn't it?

"I think we need to meet right away."

The next evening, I sat with the other Grannies in Agatha's living room waiting for Elfy to arrive so the meeting could begin. Despite the light banter and enthusiasm, there was a tension in the room as everyone stole glances towards the door.

"I wish she'd come, for Chrissakes." Joey put into words what was on everyone's mind.

"If she'd come, we could start." Grace bit her lower lip.

"If she'd come, we could relax," I added sighing.

"I telephoned six times," Estelle said, her eyes as big as eggs.

"I called seven," Joey said.

"Five times," added Grace softly. "Why isn't she answering?"

The image of Elfy in a drunken stupor staggered around the room like a ghost, frightening all of us.

With a great heave of her chest, Agatha finally spoke. "I tried telephoning, too. Then I decided to find out just what was going on." She fingered her gold necklace. "I went to her house. Of course, she wouldn't come to the door, although I rang the bell several times. I knew she was in there, so I finally peeked in through the window." She paused and swallowed. "There she was, sprawled on the floor." Agatha picked a piece of lint from her sweater and flicked it away. "I told her about the meeting tonight, but she just snapped at me to go away. I think it's fairly obvious she's into the sauce again."

I looked around at the other desolate faces. Every fibre in my body resisted the truth of Agatha's news. I knew it was rare for someone to stay off alcohol on the first try, but still, I had hoped. I had justified my hope by telling myself that Elfy's problem wasn't severe and that she had a strong will. Now, I realized I had told myself a lie.

The fact of Elfy's relapse seemed undeniable now. We were going to have to face it.

"Let's get on with the meeting," I said, feeling an ache in my chest. I didn't see the point of talking about Elfy anymore. It hurt too much and with the community meeting only days away, there were too many other things we needed to decide, such as who was going to cover all of Elfy's jobs.

Seeing a few nods of agreement, I gave a formal update on Charlie's condition, reporting the latest news that if he kept improving, he might be home in a few days. There was a listless round of applause. The group then chewed over the possibility of Boyd's complicity.

"Just because he's the kind of man who could have done it, doesn't mean he did do it," Agatha argued.

"The guy's guilty. That's what my gut says." Joey clenched her jaw tightly.

"Undoubtedly," Estelle said. "But it remains to be seen whether that can be proven."

"A few days ago I had a disturbing phone call." Grace's voice quivered. "From a funeral home. Asking when they could come and pick up the body of Grace Stevens." Her lips trembled. "I said, 'But I'm Grace Stevens.' The man was horribly upset."

"What a dirty trick!" Joey snapped.

"It must have been Boyd."

"The nerve!"

"We'll teach him a thing or two – "

"Let's poison his cat."

"He doesn't have a cat."

"Slash his tires then. On that fancy truck of his."

"Slash his tires? Slash his balls!"

Laughter exploded into the room.

"What about the trees?" I called out over the noise. "Every bit of energy we spend arguing about what Boyd's done or not done is energy taken away from the tree campaign. And it's by winning the tree campaign that we're going to get him. Let's get our focus back on the campaign."

"Jessie's right," Agatha said, forging on. "Back to

business. First of all, we need to decide about the dinner. Elfreda was supposed to do her famous stew. What are we going to do now?"

"Sandwiches," Joey suggested simply. "Everyone can make a bunch and we can freeze them if we don't need them."

"I'll make cream cheese pinwheels," Grace offered.

"This isn't a garden party," Joey said.

"I like cream cheese pinwheels," Estelle said, drawing her slender neck up out of her body. She turned to me. "How's your speech going?"

The Grannies all turned to me. How could I tell them I still couldn't think of what to say? "Fine," I told them, not wanting them to worry.

We spent the rest of the evening going over details of the community dinner and meeting, as gravely as if we were planning a funeral.

Chapter 15

The day of the big community meeting, I awoke to rain. Not a light, gentle rain, but the serious, no-nonsense kind of downpour that floods the streets and keeps people inside. If this keeps up, I won't have to give my speech, I thought and immediately felt guilty.

Drearily, I stared out the window. The rain was sluicing down so heavily that there were ponds of water on the lawn. This was bad. From the look of things, all the community activities we'd planned in the park would have to be cancelled. The meeting in the hall could still occur, but its success depended upon hordes of people coming to protest. Who was going to come out in this storm?

I still didn't know what I was going to say. Maybe now it wouldn't matter. Once again I picked up a paper and pencil, waited for some inspiring thoughts, but nothing came. What was I going to do? Stand up and play the kazoo?

Charlie nuzzled my hand and I ran my open palm along his silky fur. He'd just come home yesterday and since then, we'd stuck close to each other.

I wished Elfy had been around to talk to. Only now did I realize how much I counted on the old woman. It had been days since Elfy had holed herself up in her house, refusing to see anyone. It was crazy. Once again, I debated with myself about going over and confronting her. From the sounds of it, I'd have to force my way in. She wasn't answering her door. But then what? Was I strong enough to bundle her into a car and drag her to some detox centre? If I thought it would do any good, I would have tried. But if Elfy was determined to drink, she'd find a way to escape as my mother always had.

Why couldn't Elfy have had her relapse when all this was over? Didn't she know how much I needed her, needed her humour, her courage, her support? She would know what to do about my speech.

"What am I going to say, Charlie? What am I going to say?" I wanted my speech to be extraordinary. Not for my sake, but for the trees. I wanted to be so convincing that everyone in the room would decide to support us. With expectations like that, I knew I didn't have a hope of even writing the speech, let alone giving it.

The subject was too important, my feelings too strong. There would be hostile people in the audience. What if they shouted things? Or booed me down? I trembled. I felt like a violet peeping its head up on a bowling green.

If I told the truth, my truth, I knew what would happen: I would come off looking like an extremist. It wasn't my nature to be extreme. Yet, I had to admit, that was how I was acting. Circumstances had forced me into the position where extremism was the only option.

Normally, I liked to stay clear of the collective way. Distrusting the values of the times, I'd learned to tuck what mattered to me into places far from the collective eye. Like a lone wolf, I'd found my own way. I worked independently and liked to think I had independent thoughts. And a body still alive enough to tell me what was what. Especially now that I was listening.

Like many women of my generation, I'd kept quiet. Rather than challenge, I'd simply found my own road. But my own road diverged further and further from the prevailing way. The superhighway Boyd so clearly epitomized. Boyd, the prodigal son. Purveyor of progress, profit and other profanities. Yet he was the chosen one. To challenge this, challenge it openly, as I was now considering, was an act of insurrection. And even though my mouth was willing to be an insurrectionist, my legs knew the danger and wanted to run like a rabbit.

The telephone rang. Startled, I sat and listened to it ring, too immobilized to answer. Was it the doctor's office calling to tell me the results of the tests? *Oh, God, please not that.* It was probably a client. Feeling anxious, I picked up the phone.

"Rudi!"

There was a pause. Her voice was raspy. "Can you come?"

Everything but Rudi disappeared. "Yes! I'll come right away." There was another silence. All I could hear was soft, laboured breathing, then the phone went dead.

As soon as I heard the dial tone, the day's commitments dropped over me like a net. Pacing the room, I calculated how long it would take me to get to Rudi. I might miss the community dinner, but it was possible to make it back for the meeting. Maybe. I had to take that risk. I had to go to her. She wouldn't have asked me to come unless the end was near. And from the sound of her voice, that wasn't far away.

I made a quick call to Agatha, told her what I was doing and before she could sputter a reaction, rang off.

Racing down the wet highway, it took me just under two hours to get to the house. Sombrely, Rudi's daughter let me in. "The doctor thinks she's going to be all right, but she says she's dying. I don't know who to believe."

I nodded, not trusting myself to talk, and followed Margaret's tall body up the wide staircase. Margaret opened one of the bedroom doors, let me in and closed it again. I could hear her going back down the stairs.

At first, I thought I was in the wrong room. Yes, there was an old person in the bed in front of me, but no one I knew. Rudi had a large, vibrant body. The person I was staring at was small, with shrunken, withered skin that pulled in on itself like very old fruit. How could this be Rudi?

Feeling my presence, the woman's eyes moved to me and, suddenly, the face I knew sprang towards me, a small smile rippling at the edge of her lips. I rushed to her bedside and took her hand. It felt as light as a child's. Gently, I kissed it and eased myself down so I could sit on the bed and look at her.

Despite the limpness of her demeanour, her eyes sparked with her inimitable ferocity. As usual, they held me in a grip that was physically palpable. Turning cautiously, as if the movement were painful, she lifted a finger and veered it towards the wall beside her bed. I looked up and saw my own face and those of the other Grannies grinning back at me. All our news clippings were pinned on the wall.

Her voice was weak and there was a dull, scratching sound to it like a spoon scraping the bottom of a deep, wooden barrel. "Good for you."

Tears welled in my eyes.

"Tell me – " she said, her eyes shining.

So I told her all that had happened in the last few weeks while she nodded like a pleased parent. I even told her about Harley. When I had finished, she squeezed my hand.

"I still get scared," I confessed. "Like tonight, I'm supposed to give a speech. I'm terrified."

"Nothing wrong with fear." Her voice was slow and thick, but she carried on. "That goes with living fully." She took a long breath. "Let yourself have it." She paused, waiting for energy. "Just don't let it have you." She smiled at me with amusement, then closed her eyes, obviously tired.

Rudi had a way of explaining things that no one else had. One of my tears dropped on our joined hands. How was I going to get along without her? We sat for a long time without speaking.

"Speak from the heart," she said finally, her eyes opening. "That's where your power is." Her voice was getting weaker and weaker.

I nodded and gripped her hand tightly as if I could physically hold her back from where she was going.

"It's fine." Her voice was very quiet now. Her eyes looked at me lovingly. "You'll see."

She lapsed into stillness again and I sat listening to the rhythm of her breath. The smell of tulips wafted in through the open window. I thought she was asleep when she raised my hand to her pale lips.

I tensed. Was she going to die this very moment? Surely, a person couldn't just say goodbye and die when one wanted . . .

After a few moments of sitting still, I noticed

something swirling above her head. I blinked and looked towards the window to see if some extra sunlight was coming in the room. But this light was not sunlight. It was golden-silver and seemed to be moving in a series of circles, heightening in intensity as it spun near her hair.

Amazed, I watched the spinning light become brighter and brighter as if firing itself up to full intensity. When it had reached its peak, the light began to move down Rudi's body, turning everything beneath it into a silvery translucence. At Rudi's feet, it paused as if adjusting itself, then began moving upwards. Wide-eyed, I watched as this swirling force, travelled back up, gathering her life-force as it went. When it reached the crown of her head, it hovered for a moment. In a flash, Rudi's eyes opened and there for me to see was a look of such exaltation I almost cried out. Then the light shot up and away from her body, taking the last of Rudi's aliveness with it.

I sat, incredulous. She was gone. I expected desolation but joy filled me.

Chapter 16

All the way home I was exuberant. Death was no longer a monster. The reign of terror had finally been broken. Thanks to Rudi. That had been her last gift to me. I felt deeply grateful.

As I sped north, I had an odd feeling. After Bart had died, and my father too, I hadn't been able to feel either of them in any way. That was one of the reasons I had been dreading Rudi's death. I thought she would disappear from me completely. But I felt as connected to her as if she were sitting in the passenger seat beside me.

With tears streaming down my face, I drove on. Soon, the rain thinned and the sky brightened. By the time I drove through Barrie, the grey clouds had drawn themselves back and revealed an exquisite, light blue sky. It was going to be a perfect evening. At least now, the community events would not have to be cancelled. If we lost, we would have had our hearing. Our day in court.

A breezy warmth streamed through my window and I reached my arm out into the air, feeling the wind press against my open palm. I felt as if I were ready for anything. I still didn't know what I was going to say, but it no longer mattered. I checked my watch. The Grannies would be setting up for the picnic in the park and I wondered how they were getting along without either Elfy or myself to help. I hoped they would be able to pull in others to give them a hand. They were good at getting people to do things – especially when Estelle wore her lavender talcum powder.

An hour later, when I arrived at the park, I could hardly find a place to leave the car, there were so many vehicles lining the streets. At the entrance, the Grannies had hung coloured lights and green and pink balloons. As I approached, I could see Joey and Grace, dressed in their infamous Guerrilla Granny tee-shirts, welcoming people, handing out flyers and giving away balloons. Estelle was set up at a table selling posters and calendars. I saw Agatha leading a group on a tour through the trees, her arms gesturing grandly.

Thanks to the zeal of the Grannies, there wasn't a man, woman or child in town who didn't know about the threat to the trees. And whether it was to register their support, see the trees for the last time or simply be a part of the action, people were streaming into the park from every direction.

Children came dragging tired parents, parents came dragging tired children, students came, teachers came, people from the rich area of town and people from the poor area came. The docks down by the water were jammed with the mahogany launches of cottagers who boated in by the dozens to see what was happening.

As well as those from town, the people who had come to take part in the Earth Elder Festival were also there. Although the Festival wasn't scheduled to begin until the next day, white-haired men and women were everywhere. Many of them wore bright yellow tee-shirts with the words EARTH ELDER – HANDLE WITH CARE written in big letters on the back.

"If I see one more old person with protruding blue veins I'm going to scream," Joey said as she uncovered trays of sandwiches. "Hey! Jessie. You're back." She threw her thick arms around me and gave me a powerful hug. "I told everyone you would be. I even bet Agatha a fiver. I should'a bet twenty."

The others gathered around me. "Are you all right?" Agatha asked, looking concerned.

"Yes . . . in fact, I'm very good, considering."

"Did she . . . pass on?" Grace asked softly.

I nodded and there was a moment of stillness amongst the small group of us. In the silence I felt their love and support.

Then Joey clapped her hands loudly. "Let's get this show on the road." Around her, everyone began to put trays of food out on the long tables.

"Isn't this marvellous?" Estelle said, looking out at the crowd. "The mayor is going to have to listen now."

"A politician never has to do anything," Joey said. "And listening isn't their strong suit." She cleared away a tray of sandwiches and unwrapped another. "How in heaven's name are we ever going to feed all these Earth People?" she grumbled. "Trust Elfreda to duck out just when we need her the – "

"Bitch, bitch, bitch."

We all turned. Elfy stood behind us holding a large pot which she was trying to heave onto the serving table. After she'd managed to get it there, she handed a ladle to Joey.

"What are you staring at? I said I'd make supper and I made supper. Now serve it up. And don't be stingy." She wiped her brow and moved the trays of sandwiches aside.

It was obvious from the laborious way she was moving that everything was taking great effort.

"Why don't we just leave the sandwiches?" Joey suggested, looking at Elfy. "Then people can have a choice."

"I don't want people to have a choice, that's why." Elfy heaved herself down beside me.

I grinned like a kid. Elfy looked terrible, pale and dishevelled as a dog dragged out of a sewer, but I was utterly delighted to see her.

"I know what you're thinking," Elfy said, her face yellow and ill-looking.

"No," I contested, "you know what I've been trying not to think."

"Well, Agatha then." Elfy pitched a resentful glare at Agatha who was now a distance away, talking to some people.

"You know Agatha," I cautioned. "She thinks the worst of everybody. It doesn't mean anything. What matters is whether you're all right."

Elfy softened and looked hard at me. "Yeah, I'm all right. Now. I was sick as a dog though. I haven't ever had the flu like that before. I spent the first two days hanging down the toilet and the rest sprawled out on the floor with a bucket in my hand."

"Flu? You had the flu?" I felt as if a bird had just been released from the cage of my chest.

Elfy frowned. "You thought I was on a bender."

"Why didn't you let any of us help?"

Elfy screwed up her face. "I didn't want anyone else to get it. That's all the tree campaign would have needed. A bunch of sick Grannies. Besides, if I let you in, I knew I'd have to deal with old chicken face over there and I wasn't up to it."

I laughed despite myself. I'd never thought of Agatha looking like a chicken, but with those jowls, I could see where Elfy got the idea.

"I may have been a drunk once, but I never lied about it," Elfy said bitterly. "I never tried to cover it up. That's not my style." She turned back to Joey. "Come on, ladle it out. These people are hungry. Fill them up." She stood up unsteadily. "I've got another pot of that stuff at home. I'd better go get it."

"I'll take you," I said, wanting to keep her close.

Chapter 17

As I followed Elfy through the crowds, I saw Harley leaning against a tree and smiling at me.

Elfy saw him too and turned. The old woman looked at Harley, then back at me, a tender smile softening the lines on her face.

"Go on," she said. "We've got a few minutes." Seeing me hesitate, she added, "Go! You know you want to."

Slowly, I walked over to him. He looked solid and manly standing there, a blade of grass moving between his full lips. His eyes were all over me, pulling me to him.

"Tell him I want a feather too," Elfy called and chuckled.

I moved nearer to him, feeling the steady quietness of his body as I approached. "I thought you were still away . . ."

"I was, but I heard there was this incredible woman speaking at the town hall tonight, so I rearranged things." He wrapped his arm around me and lead me down to the lake where there were fewer people. He leaned against a tree and held me close.

"Nervous, huh?"

I nodded. I wanted to grab him by the hand and run off into the woods. Never come back.

"What else?" he asked. "There's something else . . ."

I told him about Rudi and when I was finished, he hugged me happily.

"That was the other half. Remember I said there were two parts. Trusting the earth – that was the part we covered. But the other part was trusting the sky. Your friend Rudi gave you the other half." He squeezed me hard and let me go. "There's no stopping you now." Gently he touched the centre of my chest and I felt the warmth of his fingers through my clothes.

"I'll be rooting for you." Slowly, we walked back to the centre of the park. He tipped his hat to Elfy and walked off into the crowd.

Feeling a surge of excitement and power move up from the earth into my legs, I jogged over to Elfy and we left to get the rest of the food she'd prepared.

"Are you sure you're up to this?" I asked as we lifted the heavy pot from the stove at her house and started to lug it to the car. "We could just have the sandwiches."

A crooked smile captured her mouth. "And deprive people of my culinary genius? No way!"

When we were back at the park, Elfy took over from Joey, ladling out gigantic portions.

"Step right up, everyone, there's plenty for everyone," she called, like a circus hawker. Agatha cast her a disparaging look, but Elfy carried on, undaunted.

Estelle hurried over with a pile of pages in her hands. "Look at all the signatures. I think there's over two hundred here. I let the children sign too. I don't see why children shouldn't count." She showed the pages to everyone.

"And I've just sold the last of the calendars," Agatha reported, folding up an empty cardboard box. "Let's just hope we're as successful at the town hall." She cast a meaningful glance at me as if to say, "It all depends on you."

"We better start to clean up," Joey said, barging in. "We've only got an hour until the show begins." Quickly, she began clearing up. "Let's hustle."

I pitched in for a while, then headed home to change for the meeting. If I hurried, I'd have time for a shower. I was driving quickly and taking a short cut through a part of town I normally didn't pass through. A pickup truck passed me.

Was that Robyn? For a moment it felt as though my brain were in a blender. I turned to see if I could catch a better look, but the vehicle had disappeared. Too much stress, I thought to myself as I carried on home.

By the time I changed my clothes and raced over to the community hall, there wasn't an empty seat to be found and people were lining the walls two and three rows deep. Positioned at the front, between the two opposing factions, the mayor was nervously shuffling papers. His eyes darted over the mass of people. From his agitated look, he'd anticipated a quiet, businesslike meeting. The hall, however, felt like a circus. Amidst the dozens of bobbing green balloons, children were wandering among the small clumps of people who were chatting here and there around the room.

Although things looked amicable, I sensed the tension. Occasionally, a baby shrieked over the general hubbub of conversation and people's eyes were cautious and watchful.

I took my place between Elfy and Agatha at the front. Elfy still looked tired from her illness, but her face was flushed with pleasure at the huge turnout.

Agatha nodded towards a tall man in the front row. "That's Lambert Haines, head of the Cottage Association," she whispered. "I've spoken to him several times. Luckily, I was able to press our point of view that Boyd's application, however small, is merely another step in the destruction of Muskoka as we know it. Now he's firmly on our side."

I nodded my approval. When Agatha put her weight against something, it invariably gave way.

The mayor called the meeting to order. Soberly, he outlined his wish for a fair presentation of each side. He turned his head towards his right where Boyd, in an expensive dark suit, sat flanked on either side by lawyers. On the table in front of them were three shiny black briefcases, open-jawed. Boyd flashed a shiny smile as he and his cohorts were introduced.

With a decidedly perplexed expression on his face, the mayor turned to his left, where we women sat. In colourful contrast to the men, Agatha wore a blood-red skirt and matching jacket, Elfy was dressed in a sky-blue track suit and I wore forest green. As the mayor introduced us, Boyd and his men stared ahead silently, as still and certain of themselves as cogs in a wheel.

The Guerrilla Grannies were the first presenters, and once given the floor, were off like relay runners. Wanting to show people they knew their stuff, they first presented an ecologist from the University of Toronto who argued convincingly, using the latest environmental studies, why people must begin to consider trees not mere aesthetic luxuries, but prerequisites for the survival of the species.

He was followed by a tourist consultant who said matter-of-factly that the trees were a far greater economic asset to the town alive than dead. Yes, he conceded, the proposed condominiums would bring in some quick revenue, but once this revenue was spent, it would be lost forever. The park, however, might bring in tourists for generations to come. He suggested the town consider ways of utilizing the park to bring more people, something he was sure could be done easily and profitably.

When he completed his presentation, the crowd gave him long and appreciative applause. Agatha stood up and thanked him with her usual genteel aplomb and introduced a group of local school children. The Grannies had decided early in the planning stages to make their presentation as lively and as much fun as possible. Besides, since it was the town's children who would be most affected by the decision, they felt it was important to involve them.

With earnest, vulnerable faces, twenty little six-year-olds ran up onto the stage and began to recite a story about a tree and all the jobs a tree does. They told the crowd about how trees provided housing for birds and insects, how they gave shade, encouraged soil retention, produced oxygen and offered arms for swings. At the end of their recital, each child held up a cardboard letter and all the letters together spelled, "Save our trees." The crowd burst into applause as the children ran off the stage.

The room stilled in anticipation of the next speaker. I swallowed and stood up. Camera lights flashed. I looked out at the roomful of people. Some had closed, hostile faces, others were open and receptive. The faces of my supporters pressed themselves towards me with eager anticipation. They needed me to come through for them, needed me to do what it took to protect what was dear to them, the trees. My knees wobbled. I knew that if I opened my mouth at that very moment, no sound would come.

I closed my eyes, daunted by the task before me. Then I felt Rudi's warm spirit beside me. I opened my eyes, cleared my throat and began.

"Once upon a time," I said slowly, still a little breathless, "people treated children as objects. A hundred years ago, most of the children in this room would be working twelve-hour days down in the mines or in unsafe factories. In those times, children could be and often were, beaten, flogged and cruelly mistreated without anyone being able to prevent it. Most people, except for an enlightened few, wouldn't have stopped such acts, for such acts were considered normal.

"Now, of course, we recognize what an incredible resource children are." I scanned the room for Robyn and saw her standing at the back, very near the door. She was looking down at the floor.

"We recognize children as our future and know we would have no future without them. Our awareness has changed and thank goodness it has.

"At the present moment, trees have the same status as children did a hundred years ago. People can do what they want with them. Use them for pleasure or profit and no one can stop them. Because this is the norm. In fact, many people don't even bother thinking about whether this is right. Except for the enlightened few, some of whom are in this room.

"One day, however, trees will have rights too. Not human rights, but living rights. And when that time comes, it will be illegal to kill a tree for monetary gain, just as it is illegal now to use a child for monetary gain. Because by then, we'll know how important each and every tree is to our future, as we know the importance of each and every child."

I looked out to the field of faces and saw Madge. The look on her face was grave, but she was nodding pensively. This gave me the courage to go on to the next part, the hard part. If they were going to think me a lunatic, now was the time.

"Most of us imagine trees as things. Perhaps it's more convenient for us to think of them that way. Then we can do what we want with them." I swallowed. "Trees may not think like we do or feel like we do, but they are sentient beings in their own way, with a piece of their own wisdom to offer about our joint survival."

Stopping, I sipped some water and took a few breaths of air. My hand felt clammy on the glass and it took steady resolve to keep the glass from shaking. I looked up, found my eyes pulled to the back of the room. There, I saw Harley's earth-brown eyes. They wrapped themselves around me as protectively as the soil had that day in my back yard. He smiled and raised his thumbs up.

"Now, to these particular trees. The trees in this park are between eighty and one hundred years-old. They've been here longer than anyone in this room. They are a part of this town. They are part of us. Living cells, we might call them, of this community. Cutting them down means severing ourselves from our living elders. Cutting them down means hurting those men, women and children who love them and appreciate them. To create such hurt for some slim chance of monetary gain would be an act of cruelty. A cruelty that will divide us and leave scars for years to come. On the other hand, to preserve them would be an act of generosity for all."

I sat down. I was so intent on getting my breath back that I didn't immediately hear the thunderous, foot-stomping applause. I looked out and my eyes locked with Madge's. Slowly, Madge applauded.

The mayor shouted for quiet, shouted repeatedly, until finally he had to threaten to clear the hall to get the room to settle down.

Boyd's presentation began as the Grannies had expected. It was slick, sophisticated and seductive. The lights were lowered and Boyd's lawyer erected a white screen. Soon dazzling drawings of the condominiums appeared on the screen, bright and beautiful. The drawings were in colour and showed a lovely group of homes nestled into the woods.

"Amazing – the trees have suddenly reappeared," Elfy whispered to me, her voice full of sarcasm.

Using a pointer, Boyd outlined the project's benefits, emphasizing the creation of a huge spa area that would be open to everyone in the community.

"First I've heard of this," Agatha scowled as colourful drawings of a Hawaii-like spa appeared on the screen.

"Should'a known he'd have a few tricks up his sleeve," Elfy muttered. "Well, we've got sleeves too, buster."

"Why do I think this spa stuff will be forgotten as soon as the project gets approval?" Agatha said.

An odd, unpleasant smell began to permeate the room. People shifted uncomfortably in their seats and looked around. Boyd, paler now, carried on. He showed the model from different angles, suggesting to the audience that he'd consider putting in squash courts and tennis facilities. He even asked for a show of hands to see how many people would like to have such facilities in town. Some hands went up cautiously, but the smell was worse now and the mood of the crowd was restless and irritable.

Beside me, Agatha pinched her nose. Meanwhile, Boyd's lawyer began talking about the dozens of trees they planned to plant. From there, he launched into a report of the monetary benefits the project would bring to the town.

As he droned on in a facile, self-confident manner, no one was listening. The crowd was preoccupied with the putrid, ominous smell that was now everywhere. People coughed and whispered. Some left.

"What is that disgusting aroma?" Agatha demanded, her jewelled hand waving in front of her nose.

Elfy chuckled. "That's my bean dinner. My lovely little bean stew! Working its way out into the world." She hit her hand triumphantly on her leg.

"What?" Agatha hissed.

"The beans we gave out to everyone at supper." Elfy's eyes gleamed. "They weren't completely cooked, so they were nice and windy."

"My God!" I winced, holding back a laugh. "There are six hundred people in here!"

Elfy's body was pumping up and down with laughter, her chest wheezing. "Six hundred people each holding about six farts! I'll leave the math to you."

"If that's the case," Agatha said, a slow smile dawning on her carefully painted lips, "this room will be empty very soon."

"Exactly!" Elfy said.

We all stared out at the audience. Here and there quacking sounds could be heard. One person after another extracted themselves from their seats and headed for the doors. Once there was a loud, foghorn emission and people turned their heads in search of the producer.

"Mommy, it smells in here," a little boy complained from somewhere in the crowd. "Just when that man started talking."

The mother hushed the boy and the mayor intervened asking that the windows and doors be opened.

This was done, but the repugnant emissions could not be held back and the exodus continued. Soon, there were only a few dedicated folk left. By the time Boyd finished his presentation, there were only a smattering of people in the room. Sullenly, Boyd slumped back in his chair.

The disgruntled mayor stood up and brought the meeting to a close. Sourly, he told the crowd that the town would make its decision in the next few days.

Chapter 18

When the meeting was over, Harley was waiting for me. We walked home together, then took sleeping bags and lay out in the back yard. Under the silver spray of stars, we talked about the meeting.

"What a strategy." Harley chuckled. "Felix is going to get a kick out of this one. He'd like that Elfy. She's gutsy. Are you sure you're not related?"

I lay back smiling. A lovely, warm effervescence moved through my body, making me feel peaceful and elated all at the same time. Peaceful because when I'd come home, there had been a message on my answering machine saying the results of my medical tests were fine, and elated because of the success of the meeting. With a shining face and full heart, I turned my body to Harley.

The last time we'd made love, I'd been so awestruck by the pleasure of it, so starving for its delicacies, I'd feasted on him like a beggar. This time was different. I was freer. Letting my body do whatever it wanted, I heard sounds come from my throat, husky, animal-like sounds, thick with pleasure. My body, deep in its own feverish dance, moved beyond the boundaries of what I knew and flung me out into the wide-eyed wonder of the cosmos. Here, I became the blackness of the night and felt the fire of the stars in my own belly.

Harley was so tender I wanted to cry. At these moments, he touched me as if I were sacred, looking deep into my eyes as his hands stroked me. I felt cradled in the arms of some huge, magnificent being, as young and old as all time. Finally, tangled into a wondrous knot, we rolled ourselves together until we exploded into fused ecstasy.

Sometime in the night, we went into the house and slept. I dreamt I was at a banquet being held in my honour. Delicious foods were spooned into my mouth and my body thrummed with contentment.

When I awoke, Harley was gone. I knew he had to leave early and dimly remembered him kissing me goodbye. Pulling his pillow close to my naked body, I lay thinking about the day.

What now? There was nothing to do but wait for the councillors to make their decision. How long would it take? Given the way the meeting had gone, they should decide in our favour. But would they?

At least, the Earth Elder Festival was happening today, so there were many activities to distract from the waiting. The important thing would be to try to keep everyone from getting too tense. Waiting could tighten people up to a dangerous pitch. I hoped the town councillors were aware of that.

The phone rang. Here we go, I said to myself and picked it up.

"You up?" Agatha's voice bounded towards me as forcefully as a St. Bernard dog.

"Awake, not exactly up." I looked at the clock. It said seven. It felt like five.

"I think it's in the bag, don't you? The town would be a fool to ignore that amount of public pressure."

"Maybe," I said, wishing I could share her optimism.

"All kinds of people have told me they're going to telephone the mayor this morning. And send telegrams. I don't know a soul who's not on our side. It's extraordinary."

I sighed. If only change were a matter of public pressure, I thought. But in politics, no matter how many people pushed, the ball didn't necessarily move where the many hands were directing it. Money smoothed too many other pathways.

"By the way," Agatha continued, "your talk was exemplary."

I thanked her. We talked for a while about the Earth Elder Festival and agreed to see each other there later. After I got off the phone, I realized how uneasy I felt. Why?

As I got dressed, I found a note from Harley. In his dark, definite handwriting were the words, "Here's Felix's phone number. If anyone can find me, he can. Be careful. I'm with you."

Smiling, I tucked it into my pocket. Because of his craft work and involvement with other reserves, he was on the road a lot. In a way, that was good. When he came to me, he would come out of choice, not routine. I liked that.

As I readied myself for the day, I took other calls from people, congratulating me on my speech and praising my courage. Oh, the projections I was going to have to deal with. I chuckled to myself. As it was, I had to contend with people's compelling need, and now, the projections were going to be even worse.

"Well, forget it," I said aloud as if the projections

were moths flying around the room, looking for a place to land.

I put on my slippers and went out to get the morning paper. When I came back, the light on my machine was flashing. I ignored it while I read the account of last night's meeting. Not bad, I thought. The article encapsulated the main points of each argument.

"Even the photograph's not bad," I told Charlie. I looked like a woman who had something important to say. Nothing had been mentioned about the smell.

I flipped back my messages to get the one I'd just missed.

"It's Madge," the voice said, faltered. "Just wanted to talk. I'm off into town, but I'll try again later."

Thinking I might be able to catch her, I dialled Madge's number, but there was no answer. I felt relief and disappointment at the same time.

Pulled by the trees and my need to see them, I put on my sneakers and headed outside with Charlie. At the park, on surveillance duty, Elfy sat in a deck chair wrapped in an orange blanket.

"You never stop, do you?" I looked at her with real concern. Elfy looked like a bag of bones covered with flesh-coloured cling wrap.

"No, but I slow down." Elfy smiled, pointing to the chair she was sitting in. "This is the first time I've sat on the job. Usually, I'm up gabbing away to anyone who'll listen, but not this morning."

"Not to worry. You sitting down is equal to three people standing." I looked at Elfy worriedly. "Why don't you go home for a while? Let me take over. Get some rest."

Elfy scowled. "I had all the rest I wanted with the flu,

thanks. I don't want to miss anything. When you get to my age, every minute counts. I'll rest when I'm dead. Besides, I've got to do stuff for the Elder Festival."

"Well, just don't push yourself into the grave."

Elfy yawned. "I didn't get much sleep last night. Tossed around on the bed like a fish out of water." She scrutinized me. "You don't look like you got much sleep either." Her face broke into a grin. "But from that smile, your reasons for not sleeping were different from mine." Waving my embarrassment away, she added, "Some day you'll have to tell me all the juicy details. When I'm strong enough to take it." She guffawed. Then she added, "Great speech."

"It was a good meeting, wasn't it?"

"If the meeting were the deciding factor, we'd be laughing."

"Agatha thinks we've won."

"So do a lot of people," Elfy agreed. Now her eyes leapt to mine.

"And if we haven't?" I searched the lines of Elfy's face, looking for the answer.

"We'll see, I guess." Elfy shrugged and turned away, casting her glance back into the trees.

Her ominous tone made my stomach tighten. Just how far was this old woman prepared to go?

"I guess that's the big question," Elfy said, reading my mind. "Just how far are we willing to take this thing?"

"Hopefully that's a question we're not going to have to face," I said. "If the town decides in our favour . . ."

"It's not going to – you know that. So, you'd better think about what you're going to do. We all better think about what we're going to do. Because whatever is going to happen is going to happen fast. There won't be time to think."

We were silent for a long time. Our silence was interrupted by two grey-haired women walking towards us, arm in arm.

"Excuse me," the one with bright, shining eyes said. "Is this where the Festival is going to be?"

"Over there." I pointed to the area. "It starts at ten."

"We're from Oshawa," one of them said. "But when we heard about this, we just got on the bus and came right along. It's just so exciting." They picked up their pace towards the park.

Elfy winked jovially and folded up her blanket. "Maybe I will go home and get a bit of shut eye. I won't be able to party all day if I'm as tired as this."

I pulled the old woman to me and gave her a hug. She felt unbelievably frail and little. I tried to pour some of my energy into her skinny little body.

Over the next hour, the preparations for the Earth Elder Festival moved into full swing around me. Dozens of old people, some familiar, most not, scurried around, setting up chairs and speaking platforms, microphones and projectors. As I watched, booths were erected, a huge food tent went up and two very agile old ladies with visors over their eyes strung a long banner with the words "First Earth Elder Festival" between two trees out by the road.

There was an air of expectancy as the old people got things ready. Sitting beside the area where they were setting up, I couldn't help but notice the easy way the seniors worked together. There was much laughter and amiable joking.

A bald man with a thick white moustache and bushy

eyebrows brought a tray of coffee around to people. When he came my way, I asked him where he was from.

"Medicine Hat, Alberta," he answered, dimples erupting on his face as he smiled.

"You've come all the way from Medicine Hat?"

"Sure did. I've a sister in Peterborough, so it was a good excuse to see her. I have a little camper van so I'm like a turtle with his home on his back – I can go anywhere. This sounded too good to miss. I got in last night. Just in time for the town meeting. That was some speech."

"Thanks."

"Hey, John, how about some of that coffee?" someone called.

John waved and turned back to me. "How long do you think the town's going to take to make the decision?"

I shrugged. "By tonight, I hope." I frowned, realizing the town could take as long as it wanted.

"I sure hope they make the right one." He shook his head appreciatively. "These trees are beauties, all right. Real beauties." He turned and took his tray of coffee to those who awaited him.

As the hours passed, more and more people poured into the park. Out by the road, I could see Joey and Grace hawking people in as they walked with their sandwich boards. I was glad when Estelle came to do her stint at surveillance and I was free to wander around.

By late morning, I stood with the swelling crowd, waiting for the opening ceremonies to begin. Because of my involvement with the tree campaign, I hadn't had much time to find out what Elfy and her friend, Ruth, had been organizing. After that, when Elfy had dropped out of circulation, I had assumed the event would fall by the wayside. Ruth, however, had obviously kept right on working, for the park was jammed.

A microphone reverberated with a few electronic whines and Elfy climbed on to the platform at the front of the crowd. "Hi," she called and the crowd answered back with an even louder "Hi!" Elfy grinned. "Good thing I had my hearing aid turned down." She gripped the podium and surveyed the crowd. "I can hardly believe we've pulled this thing off." Some people in the crowd chuckled.

"First of all, as some of you may know, this whole Earth Elder Festival arose out of another ecological event that is still going on. Probably by now you've seen some of us walking around with tee-shirts saying 'Guerrilla Grannies'." She turned and showed the crowd the back of her tee-shirt. People whistled and clapped. "These Grannies, and I am proud to say I am one, got together to save – " she turned her head to the adjoining park, and everyone in the audience turned with her – "to save those magnificent trees over there."

"Through a lot of hard work, we've managed to put up some pretty hefty resistance! By getting community support, we were able to force the town to grant us a public meeting, which, for those of you who have just arrived, was last night. The town is considering their decision at this very moment. As soon as we know, we'll make an announcement."

She paused and looked out at the crowd. "Early in the tree saving campaign, the Grannies realized how perfect older people are for these kinds of ecological actions. We, as older people, are unique. We have the one thing that almost no one else has in our society: time. And if there's one thing these actions require, it is that very thing: time. Time to work through red tape, time to do petitions, time to talk to people. Making change requires time.

"We have another quality also. We remember what it was like before. We remember the smell of clean air. We remember the taste of unpolluted water, we remember the sound of bird song." There was a burst of applause from the audience. "We are the last people on the planet to know what a healthy world feels like. We know the value of it. We know how important that world is to the survival of our grandchildren.

"So our hope in getting this little shindig going was to help older people realize their incredible potential for making change. We also wanted to let you know what kinds of actions are desperate for your help. We want to get you involved. Because, before all this craziness in the world today, old people were respected, were considered wise and valuable. They were elders. We want that respect back. The earth needs us to have that respect back. As Earth Elders, every senior citizen in this land could make a difference. In fact, in my opinion, I think it's the Elders who are going to save the day."

"Now, here's the main organizer of this Festival, Ruth Barker, who's going to tell you more."

Applause burst from the audience, but Elfy paid little attention and turned to draw a heavy woman with a warm, but fierce face up to the microphone. Ruth described various environmental challenges in Canada and what small groups of Earth Elders could do about them. When she was finished, she asked those who were interested in signing up for various action projects to come and see her.

I was pleased to see people making their way towards the front. Wanting to take a look at the various displays, I wandered over to the periphery of the park. There were booths selling Earth Elder tee-shirts, books on aging and agism, and other things like buttons that said 100% RECYCLED.

As I looked around, Joey came up behind me. "Why did the old person cross the road?"

I shrugged. "Tell me."

"Because she forgot she'd crossed it already." Joey groaned. "I've heard more jokes about old people today . . ."

"I didn't know there were jokes about old people."

"Apparently," Joey said, leading me towards a park bench. She sat heavily. "Any word yet?"

"Not that I've heard." I felt queasy in my stomach and checked my watch. "It's three. It can't be much longer now."

"Estelle called the town a while ago and was basically told to bug off. Politely, of course."

"Maybe we could walk over there in an hour or so," I suggested.

Joey grimaced. "The place is crawling with reporters. I passed by there on my way over here and one of them ran up to me and wanted to know what our plan of action was if the town turns us down."

"What did you say?"

"I told them we're going to bomb the courthouse." Joey snapped her teeth together angrily. "What do you think I said?" Her nostrils flared. Then, looking chagrined, she said, "I said nothing. Just 'no comment'." She rolled her dark, brooding eyes towards me. "But what are we going to do?"

I bit my lip. "Let's just hope we aren't faced with that decision."

"Shouldn't we have a plan?"

Elfy came up behind us. "Hey, there's a woman talking about agism over there. Let's go and hear her." Grateful for the distraction, I followed Elfy and soon we were listening to a very tall woman talk.

"How do you know if someone's prejudiced against old people?" the woman asked, looking out into the crowd.

She adjusted her glasses and answered her own question. "They help you across the street even when you're on your skate board."

A roar of laughter erupted from the crowd. "I heard another joke the other day," the woman continued. "Someone asked me how two old people make love. Here was the answer: they take their nitroglycerin, cover themselves with lubricant, turn up their hearing aids, watch a few hours of pornographic movies to warm themselves up, then fall asleep and dream about it."

There were uncertain rumblings from the crowd.

"Just think of the assumptions in that joke, which, by the way, was told to me by someone under fifty." She paused. "Now, I like a good joke, but I'm getting tired of the way people think of older people – as weak-bladdered, dribbling, forgetful, doddering, half-blind, slow driving, impotent, dentured and brittle-boned fools.

"Sure, old people have their share of problems. But to be defined by our problems and all be painted with the same brush is discrimination! What about all the older men and women who don't fit these limiting definitions? What about the growing number of seniors who run marathons? Or seniors like Colonel Sanders, who decided he couldn't live on his old age pension and with only a chicken recipe as an asset, became one of the most successful entrepreneurs in history?

"There are many examples. Famous people like Albert Einstein, Georgia O'Keefe, Carl Jung and Picasso are just a few of many people who have made some of their greatest contributions in the latter years of their lives.

"And then there are people like Hilda Crooks, who at the age of seventy, decided to become a mountain climber. Today, at ninety, she has scaled some of the highest peaks in the world and is the oldest woman ever to climb Mount Fuji.

"Isn't it time we stopped thinking of older people as decrepit? We are, or can be, a powerful force in the world. We need to take charge of our lives and take our places as vibrant, powerful people. Thank you."

The crowd broke into tumultuous applause the minute the woman was finished talking. I looked around. Throngs of old people were smiling exuberantly and nodding.

"Good stuff, eh?" Joey said, rubbing her legs with her wide hands.

"I'll say," Elfy agreed. "But it's not just young people who have to change their attitudes. I gave a copy of a pamphlet entitled, 'Sex in the Seventies' to a friend. She thought it was a historical review, not an article about sex and seventy-year-olds."

"Hey, I like this!" Joey said. We were out of the tent now and surrounded by more things to look at. Joey pointed at a tee-shirt that said EIGHTY AND AWESOME. She motioned the rest of us over to the booth.

"You're not eighty, yet," Elfy snapped.

"Give her something to look forward to," I suggested.

"Then, how about this one?" Joey said, holding up another. On this one were the words: Baby Centurion.

I smiled. "I like this one the best." I read the words on the shirt out loud. "I have eaten 90,000 meals, laughed 10,000 times, slept 240,000 hours, read 2,000 books, paid over $500,000 in taxes and spent 175,000 hours with children! Respect me. I'm your average 80-year-old."

"HA!" Elfy cried, digging into her pocket. "That's one I have to own." When she made her purchase, we moved on.

The next booth was manned by John, the person who had given me a coffee earlier in the day.

"What are you selling?" I asked.

"Nothing. I'm gathering names for tree-protection legislation, if you want to sign on the dotted line."

"The Grannies were talking about doing that," I said, signing the petition. "We just never had time to get it going. Good for you, John."

"Any news?" Estelle asked, joining us.

I shook my head and the two of us wandered through the park. My stomach was tightening and tightening as if preparing itself. Why was it taking so long?

Spotting us, Grace came hurriedly over.

"Any news?"

"No news is good news," Estelle trilled.

The five of us moved as a group now, sticking together like nervous puppies. We had just emerged from a small tent where we'd seen a documentary film about trees in the rain forest when a reporter rushed over.

"Mrs. James! Mrs. James! What are your plans now?"

I felt a wave of confusion. Something wasn't making sense. "Until we hear from the town . . ." Elfy squeezed my arm hard.

"I think the reporter has news for us," Elfy said firmly. "Let's listen."

"Haven't you heard?" the reporter shouted. "The town has rejected your proposal in favour of the developer's!"

I tried to swallow but couldn't. It was as if someone had sucked the very juices out of me. I felt old and dried up. The reporter pressed closer, but I was saved from speaking by the arrival of Officer Tamlin, who walked directly over to us with a grim, but determined expression on his face.

"We've heard." Joey crossed her thick arms over her wide chest.

"I got to tell you anyway," he said. "The town has decided to support Mr. Murdon's project as planned. All persons are required to vacate the city park by nine pm. By order of the town."

"But the Festival – " Elfy argued.

"If you will check your permit, ma'am, you'll see that it expires at that time."

"I know that," Elfy said. "But we need time to pack everything up and . . ."

Tamlin was not listening. Having done his unpleasant duty, he turned and left.

"They're clearing the park so they can take the trees down," Agatha said flatly.

A crowd gathered around us and the ring of people thickened as more and more people heard the news. Comments rumbled through the crowd.

"I'm not going anywhere." Joey sat down on a bench obdurately. "This is my park, too."

"If they want us out, they can drag us out," a man said, positioning himself beside Joey.

I was quiet, stunned by how quickly things were escalating. Before I knew it, people were piling up chairs, overturning platforms and making a huge barricade.

"Jessie, do something!" Agatha hissed at me. "This is getting out of hand."

I shook my head. The speed and ferocity of the action around me had a life of its own.

Chapter 19

After the barricade was up, people made forays out to gather necessities. Elfy was climbing over the tables to do a relay when I caught the back of her shirt. "Where are you going?"

"Home to get blankets. We could be spending the night here."

"If you bring blankets," I speculated, "more people will stay. And the more people stay, the more this thing will escalate."

"Maybe it needs to escalate," Elfy said and hurried on. Others joined her.

Soon, heaps of camping equipment, blankets and ground sheets appeared. Boxes of food were brought over from the Festival's food tent and stacked in a corner.

"We've got food for days," Joey said, leaning against several large coolers filled with leftovers. "So the basics are covered."

Amazed, I watched as people arranged the food and equipment. After a while, someone lit a small cook stove and cups of hot chocolate were passed around to the forty or fifty protesters. This was followed by a tray of chunky cheese pieces and assorted fruit.

"I feel like I'm at Girl Guide camp again." Estelle

cheerfully pulled a red Hudson's Bay blanket around her legs. "Isn't that sunset marvellous?"

I looked at the pinkening sky but was too preoccupied to enjoy it. If the sun were setting, that meant Tamlin would soon be back. Would he come with reinforcements? Just how many officers could a small town like ours muster? I shivered. Things were coming to a head and I was frightened.

Nervously, I thought back to protests I'd seen on television. Visions of police billy-clubbing protesters and dragging them to paddy wagons filled my mind. Is that what was going to happen here? I'd already been to jail once this month. I didn't want to go again.

At precisely nine o'clock, Tamlin returned. In a terse, determined tone, he ordered the crowd to vacate the park immediately. Around me, people booed him loudly.

I stood up and looked over the pile of upturned tables and chairs to see if I could talk to him personally. After all, the two of us liked and respected each other. But the face I encountered had hardened and was pulled into a mask of resolute anger. He stared at me as if I were the enemy.

Feeling weak in the knees, I sank to the ground. The battle lines were drawn. I was now no longer someone Tamlin knew, someone who had a heart and a body just like him. I had become the opposition. I shuddered. I wanted to shout at him, "It's me. It's the same old me," but I knew it would be useless.

I watched as Tamlin strode off. He walked with the weighty confidence of someone who knows he's got bigger guns to rely on.

"What's he going to do?" Grace asked. There was a worried tremor in her voice.

"Nothing, tonight," Joey answered, taking a large bite of a sandwich.

John stroked his white moustache and spoke matter-of-factly. "In the morning, they'll come with as many reinforcements as they need to move us out of here."

"What if we refuse to move?" Estelle's voice was strained.

"Then they'll drag us out, limb by limb," John said, inducing sober quietness all around him. "I was involved in the protests against the logging companies in British Columbia. The police were merciless."

Like a terrified frog, fear jumped from person to person in the crowd.

"But we're not a bunch of long-haired hippies," Agatha protested.

"Neither were they," John said. "There were lots of older people there too, and they were treated just as roughly as everyone else."

"I'm glad there was no discrimination," Joey said wryly.

"What do you mean, 'roughly'?" I asked. I wanted to know what to expect.

"They didn't beat us, if that's what you're worried about," John said. "There were too many news people around. But they did forcibly remove us. I had an arm badly wrenched. Being yanked around by the cops is not my favourite sport. They make sure it's not your favourite sport either."

I winced. Beside me I could feel Agatha bristling.

"Did they use tear gas or horses or anything like that?" Joey asked.

"No," John replied, "they didn't have to. We weren't

rioting. We were just there, obstructing. The same as we're doing here." He shook his head. "I think they hate that the most – when people don't riot. It makes it harder on them. They have to face you, human being to human being."

"You lost, didn't you?" a voice asked from the crowd.

John shrugged. "It depends how you look at it. No, we didn't stop them from felling trees every day. But we slowed them down. And we showed the logging companies that they can't just do whatever they want, whenever they want. We showed them that there are growing numbers of people who are saying 'NO' and who are willing to put their bodies where their words are. To me, that's a victory."

There was a long silence. People pulled their blankets tighter and didn't look at each other.

"I'm frightened," Grace whispered.

"Me, too," I replied, realizing that this was probably the last thing Grace wanted to hear. I put my arm around her. She did not look well. Suddenly I felt angry. It was ridiculous that we should be forced into these extremes. Why couldn't we work this out peacefully? I thought about Martin Luther King and the battle for racial equality. I thought about the skirmishes the natives were having in order to hold on to their land and values. I thought about the fights women had fought. All this fighting about basic rights. It was crazy.

"Surely there's a civilized solution," Agatha said.

"We're beyond civilized," Joey said.

"I'm never beyond civilized," Agatha retorted.

"Too bad for you," someone muttered.

Agatha scowled but was quiet.

Elfy spoke. "Hey, everyone, relax! Or I'm going to pee in my pants."

A titter of laughter rippled through the crowd.

I felt deeply troubled. Civil disobedience on this scale was new to me. I didn't want to reject it as an option because it was unknown, but never before had I been involved in something where the potential for destruction was as great. But the times were changing. Maybe actions like this were going to become the norm. What other options did people have?

"I just wish I knew what we were in for," someone said from the crowd.

"I can tell you that." Agatha's voice was hard. "We're going to spend a miserable night here, not getting any sleep. At the crack of dawn, the police are going to come and forcibly remove us. Some of us will be hurt. All of us will go to jail. While we are in jail, they will come and cut the trees down and all this will have been for nothing."

"It won't be for nothing. We will have made our point." John's voice was short and clipped.

Agatha sighed deeply and looked around uncertainly. "I think we've already made our point about the trees. We've taken this as far as it can go. It's time to pack up and go home before someone gets seriously hurt."

"Eternally optimistic." Joey glared at Agatha.

Agatha came over and wedged herself closely beside me. "Call this off," she hissed. There was an agitated, fearful grate to her voice. "I don't think people have any idea what they're getting themselves into."

I put my arm softly around her shoulders to comfort her, but Agatha stiffened. I could see the sparkle of tears brimming in her eyes.

I looked at her blankly. "I couldn't call this off if I tried."

"But they'd listen to you! The Grannies would anyway. Except for Elfreda. But the rest would." Her eyes were large with fear. "We're in danger here!"

I felt a churning confusion inside my body. Too much was happening too fast. On the one hand, things had gone far enough. We'd done what we could to save the trees. Continuing would only put everyone at risk. The Grannies, tough as they were, could be easily hurt and I felt protective of them. This part of me thought I should stand up and tell everyone to go home.

Another part of me wanted to take things to the finish, to follow what we'd set in motion and see where it took us. There would be something fulfilling about going for it right to the end and not giving up.

But how would I feel if someone got hurt? I pictured a fragile body crushed by an overturned picnic table. What if something like that happened to one of the Grannies? If something like that happened, I'd never be able to forgive myself.

Beside me, Agatha stood up abruptly. Her large frame cast a huge shadow behind her. She carefully folded the towel she'd been sitting on. Sensing the tension, the people around her watched nervously.

"I don't know about everybody else," she said, "but I have no intention of being manhandled by the police. I'm going home. If the rest of you have any sense, you'll do the same." She looked piercingly at me, then eyed Grace. "I think you'd better come with me, Grace."

Grace's thin lips pressed together anxiously. She looked over at me.

"Should'a known you'd – " Joey hissed at Agatha.

I silenced her with my hand and nodded at Grace. "Remember our agreement: everyone has to do what's right according to their own conscience." I looked around the crowd. "If anyone else wants to go, they should feel free to do so."

Elfy, her face more serious than I'd ever seen it, nodded in agreement. We all watched Agatha and Grace pick their way through the sprawling bodies and climb carefully over the picnic tables.

The rest of us sat despondently. Trying to lighten the mood, John took some kindling and dead wood he'd collected earlier and began to make a fire.

"Does anyone care if we break another ordinance?" he asked. Hearing no objection, he lit a match.

I watched as the small flame flickered, caught the twigs above it and flared into a crackling fire. Soon the flames of the small fire leapt up over the twigs, sending a reddish glow to all the faces around. The last time I'd been around a fire, it had been with Harley. I wanted Harley here now. He'd know how to handle this.

"Look what I found." Joey held up a bag of marshmallows. The mood of the group lightened as people found sticks and began to roast the marshmallows. A transistor radio was turned on and the sound of a jazz saxophone filled the air. As the hours passed, some people lay back and tried to sleep, others talked. But still, an agitated restlessness remained.

I shut my eyes. Maybe Agatha was right. Maybe we should all leave while leaving was still possible. If only I could think. Inside my brain, everything felt so wound up, it was hard to get my mind to function properly. If only I could talk to Harley.

Miserably, I lay back and stared into the darkness. After a while, the radio was turned off and a deathly silence fell over the group. I wished I could sleep like the others around me, but I was too keyed up. Finally I flung back my blanket.

"I'm going for a walk," I whispered to Elfy. "I've got to think."

The old woman pushed herself up on one elbow and searched my face. Reaching her hand forward, she gently brushed the hair out of my eyes.

"I'm just so keyed up . . ."

"Me too," Elfy confessed, speaking softly so she wouldn't wake the others. "But the way I figure it, I'd rather be out here, going for something I believe in, than knitting doilies in an old folk's home. Even if the worst happens, I'd rather die here than kick the bucket because there's nothing worth living for."

"Oh, Elfy, don't talk like that."

"Well, it's true." She grinned. "I feel alive out here. Alive. Like I'm doing something that really matters. How many old people can say that, eh?"

"She's right," Joey said from under a big hump of blankets. "Think of all those old fogies lying in their beds right now, unable to sleep. I don't care if I sleep. This is so exciting."

"But aren't you scared?" I asked. "What if things get crazy and something terrible happens?"

"I'm not afraid of dying, if that's what you mean," Joey replied. "Until I do, I'm going to stuff as much into living as I can. I've never been part of a protest before."

"Maybe in the next protest," Estelle said, pulling her long neck out of a sleeping bag, "we can have better sleeping accommodation."

I looked at Estelle with concern. "I'm worried about you facing all this." Although I didn't say it, I wished she'd left with Agatha and Grace.

"I wouldn't miss it for the world," Estelle said, then added quietly. "I had a dream a few weeks ago that my sister was waiting for me. She passed away five years ago. I think about her when I get frightened."

The four of us lapsed into silence. I tightened the laces on my shoes and got ready to get up.

"Want company on your walk?" Elfy asked.

I shook my head, patted Elfy's shoulder and climbed over the barricade. When I was under a street light, I checked my watch. Four a.m.. I walked along the deserted streets until I reached my house. Charlie would need to go out. It had been hours since I'd been home and I had no idea when I'd be back again. I knew I couldn't count on Robyn to take care of him.

Charlie was waiting for me at the door. Not bothering to turn on the lights, I knelt down and petted him while he whined and wiggled his greeting.

"Were you worried about me?" I crooned at him, trying to settle him down. "It's all right, yes, it's all right. I know, you've been wondering where I was." I glanced longingly towards the bedroom. How I yearned to crawl into bed, pull the covers over my weary body and forget about the world.

Should I try and call Harley? If I had known I could have reached him, I would have tried. But he was out of town still, so even if I could have called him, I wouldn't have been able to see him. And seeing him was what I needed.

Hearing a door close softly, I turned in alarm. A dark figure moved towards me in the blackness. I opened my mouth to scream when light erupted into the room. In rumpled clothes, Robyn stood by the lamp.

"Mother, what are you doing?"

"What are you doing?" I countered. I turned to see if I could catch a glimpse of the car I heard driving away, but couldn't. What was going on? From the closed expression on Robyn's face, I knew she would tell me nothing.

I made myself more conciliatory. "I was down at the park. We're making a last ditch effort to save the trees."

Robyn flounced down in a chair. Her cheeks were flushed. Charlie walked over to her tentatively. She petted his head lightly.

"To think anyone would try to poison you!" She said to him as she gave me one of her "How stupid can you get" looks.

"Yes, imagine me thinking such a thing of a nice man like Boyd," I replied, copying her insouciant tone.

Oblivious of the sarcasm, Robyn's eyes roamed around the room. "Boyd's bought a number of my photographs today," she said casually. "He thinks they're very artistic."

"They are!" I answered, feeling like a pinball machine with alarms and buzzers going off inside my body.

"He wants to put them in the foyer of the new condo."

"The tree photographs?" I was incredulous. "Not the tree photographs!" My voice sounded pleading even to my own ears.

"Yes, the tree ones." Robyn's eyes glided towards me, then careened on past.

"You'd let him do that? For God's sake, Robyn!" How could she do such a thing? It didn't make sense. I blinked a few times as if I were looking at a picture with a piece missing.

Trying for a reasonable tone, I said, "Of course, you can do with those photographs whatever you like, but Boyd is a smart man. He's used to getting what he wants. And he'll do whatever he can to get it."

"I don't think you know Boyd, mother."

"Oh, no?" A stream of heat shot into my face. "I know things about Boyd that would make your hair stand on end. Mean things. Things he's done to me and to people I know."

Robyn stared at me, momentarily abashed. She tossed her hair back. "You're just prejudiced."

"Of course, I'm prejudiced!" I slammed back. "What am I supposed to do, smile while he destroys things I love? Robyn, he's going to destroy those very trees your photographs say you love."

"You make him out to be a monster, mother." Robyn waved her hand dismissively.

I hooted my outrage. "What do you think, that people who do terrible things are terrible people?" I looked at her hard. "They aren't. They're people, just like us, even the worst of them, the Stalins and Hitlers of the world! Do you think *they* didn't have people they loved, that they didn't bring flowers to their mothers or stroke their children's heads? That the man who raped you didn't have brothers and sisters or have friends that thought he was a nice guy? Oh, Robyn, they're people. Like us. People who do good things and bad things. But if they do bad things and we let them, they become even more dangerous.

"One rip-off leads to another, until ripping off becomes a way of life. Like it is with nature now.

"Sure you want to sell your pictures. And Boyd wants to put up condominiums. And Madge wants to get laid. But what's the price tag? Is it worth selling your pictures if it means destroying some hundred-year-old trees? Is it worth having condominiums if it splits this town apart? And yes, Madge is getting sex, but with a man like Boyd, is it worth the price?"

I noticed the distress on Robyn's face and, thinking I was finally reaching her, I carried on. "How can we sustain life if we're willing to damage it? Or stand by and let someone else damage it? That's what we do. But when something's wrong, whether it's ripping sex off a woman or trees from a park, it's wrong. I can't pretend it isn't. I won't pretend it isn't. They can call me crazy and lock me away, but I can't lie to myself."

My legs twitched. I had to get back to the park. My course of action was as clear as if it had been lit with a spotlight. Yes, I wanted to save the trees, but whether that was possible or not didn't change the most important thing: I had to be true to myself and try. If I got hurt, so be it. As for the others, I would talk to them, make sure each of them was fully aware of the risks involved. Beyond that, my only task was to follow the truth as my heart knew it.

Aware of Robyn again, I saw her face contort. Then pain broke it open and tears dribbled from her eyes.

Feeling confused, I moved to comfort her. It had been so long, so terribly long since I had touched Robyn, and I wanted to hold her and stroke her and tell her everything was going to be all right. Years of pent-up mothering swelled in my arms towards her.

"Don't touch me," she shouted, throwing me off.

I recoiled and collapsed to the floor near her.

"You think you're so wise, don't you? You think you know everything. Well, you don't. Boyd isn't sleeping with Madge."

"But he is. I'm certain of it."

Robyn stared at me, her face a welter of hostility and hurt. "Like you were certain I was raped?"

I took a breath and held it. Staring at her incredulously, I waited for her to speak.

"He made love to me, mother. And I let him. From the time I was twelve. Over and over again. Until I was sixteen." Her voice was full of scorn. "And you were too stupid to know. You were too busy, too caught up in your fairy tales – "

No. This couldn't be true. I would have known. Surely, I would have known. My mind screamed out rebuttals, but the nausea in my stomach told me Robyn was speaking the truth.

Shame washed over me like dirty water. I thought back to my session with Donna, remembered the rage she'd felt at her mother for not protecting her. Donna's mother hadn't been there to help her know right from wrong. And I had committed the same atrocity against Robyn.

"Who was it?" I wanted to demand. My mind ransacked lists of friends, acquaintances, relatives. It must have been someone Robyn knew. In stories clients had told me, it was often a babysitter, or teacher. Someone reputable. Someone who would buy the child an ice cream and then finger them while they ate it. If these men had looked like monsters, children would know what to do. It was the incongruity that crippled response.

Neither of us spoke. Slowly I saw boxes of light appear on the carpet. The day was dawning. I knew I should get back to the trees, but I couldn't move. Guilt immobilized me. I should have known. I should have been there to help her, to protect her. The enormity of my failure flooded through me. In the turbulent swell of my anguish, a realization splashed into my awareness.

"Boyd. It was Boyd!"

"Your favourite person, mother. All those swimming lessons you paid for . . . Didn't you ever wonder why I got out so much later than the others?"

Hatred. For the first time in my life, I felt hatred. It boiled in my belly and for a moment, I thought I was going to fall into it and never come out. But my need to understand held me back. "You told me he was giving you special coaching. Because you were so good . . ." As soon as I said the words, I realized how stupid they sounded.

"Yes, you always taught me I was special. And Boyd made me feel that way. When he told me how special I was that he wanted to touch me, I believed him. And it made me feel free."

"Free?"

"Free of you."

Her words hit hard. I dropped my face to my knees, trying to hold back my emotions. There was still more I needed to know. I raised my head. "What happened that day?"

In a voice full of pain, she told me. "Boyd broke up with me. He said we had to stop seeing each other. People were getting suspicious, he said." Her voice faltered. "I grabbed at him and he didn't like it. He roughed me up. When I came home, Dad wanted to know why I was such a mess. He was the one that used the word rape. I went along with it."

"You went along with it," I repeated quietly.

"Then I kept seeing him with other women. I didn't know what to do. I had to get away. That's why I left. The day after I was sixteen and it was legal."

"I thought he'd write and tell me to come back." Anger thickened her voice. "But he didn't write. So I stayed away. When I came back, I thought it was all over. Then he wanted to see me again. He told me he'd been waiting. That Madge was just a friend."

As I watched the tears stream down Robyn's face, my own grief came tumbling down. An image of Robyn at twelve came into my eyes. So small and fragile. Naive. And I had kept her naive. I had set her up to rebel against me. She had to act out to feel that she was growing up.

I had to talk. I had to explain. If that were possible. I began slowly, grappling for words as I went. "When you were little, I gripped on to the two of you kids like handrails. I didn't want you to grow up because I knew that when you did, you'd leave me. You kids and Bart were all I had and I didn't know how I would live without you. That was wrong. Very wrong.

"But after you left, and Bart died, I had to face it . . ." I hesitated. Why was it so hard to tell one's children your blunders? Yet how could I expect to learn about Robyn if I didn't let her learn about me? No, this was not the time to hold back. "I had a sort of breakdown."

I stopped talking, remembering that terrible time.

Robyn's eyes were wide. "A breakdown?" Her voice was soft with surprise.

I nodded.

"Did you drink?"

"No – thank God. I got help before it got to that. I just couldn't get out of bed. For almost three months, I stayed in my bedroom, frightened of my own shadow."

Robyn was quiet. Finally, she asked, "What got you going again?"

There it was, that softness in her voice. It helped me go on. "Rudi. It was Rudi. She mothered me. I didn't know about good mothering – I'd never had it myself. That's why I couldn't give it to you. I overprotected you. And in overprotecting you, I ended up not protecting you at all."

I turned and looked at her. "Robyn, I'm sorry. So very, very sorry. What I did was unconscionable."

No longer able to hold back the tears, I put my head on my arms and cried. I cried for all the years Robyn had been away, I cried for the inadequate way I had mothered her and for all that she had been through. I cried as I have never cried before. As I cried, Robyn's hand tentatively reached out and touched me. Her hand had forgiveness within it.

We held each other and for a moment the past disappeared. I could smell the apple aroma of her shampoo and feel the fine bones of her hand. My breathing calmed as we leaned trustingly against each other.

There was a banging at the door. Startled, we both looked up. The room was bright and I realized that it was fully morning. The clock said it was almost eight. The front door burst open and Madge stood looking at us, her chest heaving as she fought for breath.

"They're going to move into the park. Boyd and the police. Right now."

"Why are you telling me?"

Madge looked at me intensely. "I don't know. Boyd would hurt me if he knew."

I ran out leaving the Madge and Robyn to face each other.

Chapter 20

I expected the scene at the park to be even more tense and grim by the time I returned. As I came around the corner, however, I saw red and yellow balloons tied to the trees. Children were throwing balls and trailing balloons on long strings behind them. Was I in the wrong park? The gayness of what I saw confused me. What were the Grannies up to now?

As I came closer, I saw that someone had organized the tables in a large circle like those the settlers arranged with their covered wagons when threatened by attack. I could see the Grannies and the Elders in the centre of it, serving out some sort of food. It looked more like a country fair than a protest.

Elfy threw her arms around me. "You're back!" She drew me over to the circle of tables. "We decided to lighten things up. For a minute there, it looked like we were back in the sixties!"

Joey made a fist and pumped it in the air. "Whuuu-huuu."

"Great. Boyd's on his way with the police and you're having a party." I wanted to scream at somebody. Feeling Elfy's eyes scrutinizing me, I stomped off. "What are all these children doing here?" I sounded as grumpy as I felt.

Estelle looked at me curiously and flipped some

pancakes onto a plate. "We asked our grandchildren for breakfast. Some of them brought friends," she answered. "It's going to be terribly difficult to get us all out of here. We don't want to make it too easy to close us down."

Seeing Agatha glide by with a tray full of food, I stared at her. "I thought you and Grace left?"

Agatha shrank from the harshness of my voice but said, "We came back for the pancakes. But we're leaving when the police come, that was our agreement, right, Freda?"

Elfy smiled. "And you're not going to let me forget it, are you?"

Agatha took a plate of pancakes and began passing them to the kids.

Joey poured a glob of lumpy batter into a frying pan and set it over the camp stove. She passed me a plate. "Better get something into yourself. This could be a long day." Worry pulled at her mouth. "You all right? You're white as a ghost."

"No, I'm not all right," I said, skulking off with the plate of food I had no intention of eating. A child ran past with a red balloon, but all I could think about was Boyd coming on to Robyn. She had only been a child when he'd started at her. Wasn't that illegal, having sex with a minor? Of course, it was. Even if the child went along with it, it was illegal. But if I reported it to the police and Robyn wasn't willing to talk, what would be the point? Without her involvement, nothing could happen. It wasn't fair. Boyd could take whatever he wanted, whether it be a young girl's body or a park full of trees. And there wasn't a damn thing I could do about it.

As I sat festering, John came and sat beside me,

pensively sipping his coffee. "Get any sleep last night?" he asked.

Disgruntled, I shook my head. The last thing I wanted was a conversation.

Thinking my bad humour was due to lack of sleep, John carried on. "I didn't get much either." He smoothed his moustache. "Oh, well, I didn't get involved in this for the rest." He smiled. "Funny how you can put up with things and put up with things and then one day you can't."

I nodded, reluctantly loosening myself from the knot of my preoccupation.

"How did it start for you?" John asked.

"My body threw me in front of a chain saw," I answered flatly.

John chuckled. "Our bodies are pretty smart, aren't they?"

"If only our bodies could tell us what to do with bastards like Boyd."

"Isn't that exactly what our bodies are doing?" He smiled. "Come on," he coached, "don't be so glum. It's not over yet."

"No?" I challenged, nodding to the road at the edge of the park.

"Dum-da-dum-dum!" Elfy called, seeing the line of police cars approach. "Here comes the fuzz."

All the protesters stood perfectly still as a cavalcade of police cars drew up to the curb.

"Holy shit!" Joey cried.

"One, two, three, four, five, six cars and one, two, three, four, five paddy wagons." Estelle stood stiffly, as white as a stick of chalk.

"Remember," John called out warningly to the crowd. "When they move in, stop whatever you're doing and sit down. Cross your arms in front of your chest. That way they can lift you up by the elbows and it won't hurt so much. And NO resistance. Either here or later at the station. Otherwise, you're asking for trouble." John walked around the crowd, going over the instructions to all who would listen.

"What about the children?" I asked, but no one answered. All eyes were on the police.

A large policeman with the body of a wrestler stepped forward and picked up a megaphone.

"Clear the area," he shouted. "Clear the area or you will be forcibly removed."

Startled by the loud voice, the children stopped their playing and stared at the battalion of police standing at the ready. One little girl started to cry and Grace moved over to comfort her.

"Surely, they won't move in while the children are here," Estelle said, her conviction dying as she spoke.

Not wanting the children to get caught up in this, I called over to Agatha. "Could you take the children and walk them over to the other end of the park, where it's safe? That way you won't be involved and neither will they."

Agatha nodded and she and Grace spread out their arms and began to sweep the children along to a safer area.

"I want a balloon, I want a balloon," a girl in an apple green sweater cried and ran back to the food table. Graciously, Estelle leaned over and offered the child one.

As the children were being ushered away, some pickup trucks as black as hearses pulled up along the curb.

"Bastard."

Following my eyes, Joey's glance landed on my target. "Boyd!"

My hands tingled. I wanted to claw his face, scratch him, hurt him.

Boyd swung a chain saw out of the back of the truck.

I didn't know I had started to go for him until I felt Joey's strong arms yank me back. "Hold on – you're outnumbered."

"I don't care!" I said, trying to pull myself free of Joey's grip.

"But I do," Joey said softly. She did not release her hold.

The five men Boyd had brought with him arranged their chain saws in a firing line, all pointing at the protesters. Obviously, they were not going to risk another mishap and planned to take the trees down the moment the park was cleared. This time Boyd had come himself, to make sure it happened.

"All right everyone, take your positions," John warned. "They're moving in."

The Grannies and Elders sat as close as they could. Some of them shut their eyes. Others looked straight ahead without blinking.

"Come on, Elfreda," Estelle called from where she sat, near the front.

Elfy was eating a pancake. "In a minute," she replied, licking her fingers as she stared at the police.

The man with the bull horn spoke again. "You are ordered to vacate the park. Otherwise, you will be forcibly removed."

"Come on, dickheads," Joey shouted. "Get it over with."

The impenetrable line of policemen moved forward, their faces hard, riot sticks at the ready.

I felt sick and closed my eyes. In the silence, I heard a great swishing sound. It seemed that the spirits of a hundred trees had moved to join me – trees from the park, trees from around the lake, trees from other countries, gathering around me like protective relatives. Feeling their strength, I let myself relax.

Hands grabbed at me, lifting and dragging me towards the paddy wagons. Around me, I heard the groans of the others as they were pulled from their positions.

"Granny!"

Suddenly the children, who had been taken to the far side of the park, saw what was happening and ran across the grass. Frantically, they jumped on the backs and shoulders of the police and threw their arms around their legs. I saw one child jump on the back of a policeman, then pinch the man's nose and cover his mouth. The policeman was forced to let go of Joey so he could yank the small child's hands away and get some air. Joey bounded away freely.

As the police tried to recover and run after the protesters, the children shot their legs out to trip them and soon there was a mass of bodies sprawled over the lawn. I heard voices cry out in pain.

"Stop!"

I turned. The voice sounded familiar, but I couldn't attribute it to anyone I knew. It had such power. As I turned, a word slipped out of my throat like a freed bird.

"Robyn!"

There, between the protesters and Boyd, my daughter stood. Her head was held high, her shoulders thrown back and she had her feet apart as if she intended to hold her ground.

For a moment, everything stilled. Into the quiet, Robyn spoke. "Stop this, Boyd. Or I'll tell everyone everything." She tossed her hair back over her shoulders.

Boyd shifted uncomfortably, then walked towards her. As he moved, he kept his eyes on her, as though dealing with a crazed animal. Titters went through the crowd.

Although I couldn't hear what he was saying, I saw him trying to calm her. He put his hand on her arm, but she took a step resolutely away from him. He spoke, she shook her head, he spoke again. He pointed his finger at her threateningly.

"Hang in there, Robyn." I turned and saw Madge coaching from the sidelines, her hands on her hips. Her full red lips were pressed firmly together.

Robyn and Boyd both turned to see who had spoken. Robyn smiled and Boyd scowled, but kept on talking.

Joey leaned towards my ear. "What the hell's this about?"

"It's about taking a stand." I did not take my eyes off Robyn.

Elfy came and put her arm loosely around my waist. "Good for her," she whispered. "She's got more of you in her than I thought."

Boyd was grinding a foot into the ground as if trying to make something disappear. I made myself breathe. I wanted to run to Robyn and protect her, but I knew she had to do this one alone. "That woman has balls," Joey hissed.

"No, ovaries. She's got ovaries." Elfy grinned.

"For fuck's sake," Boyd suddenly shouted. The mayor,

who had just arrived, walked over to the two of them. As Robyn began to speak to the mayor, Boyd lunged towards Robyn to stop her. Furiously, Robyn shook him off.

The mayor edged Boyd away, obviously trying to cool him down.

"All right, all right," Boyd shouted and threw up his hands in disgust. "I'm outta here." Belligerently, he pushed his way back through the crowd and disappeared.

Chapter 21

I wandered into the garden. Late summer was such a rewarding time of year. Everything was ready and ripe. Nipples of raspberries, dozens of them, poked at me from their prickly reddish stems and squash vines crawled on to the paths, grasping at my legs as if trying to pull me into their tangle of growth. The tomato plants sagged with the weight of their plump, fleshy fruit and filled the air with their aroma.

Every part of the garden offered its fullness. Like a zealous lover ready to give and give again, the garden filled my harvesting baskets every day and offered more the next. Each plant had its offerings and I took them like gifts, relishing their smells and flavours at every meal. It amazed me that so much food could come from a few little packets of seeds.

I picked some black-green spinach leaves, light as air in my hands, then added some Romaine, a few tree-shaped sprigs of parsley and a handful of chives. The chives had produced lovely little mauve flower balls and I threw a few into my basket for colour as well as a couple of scarlet nasturtiums. I loved eating flowers. It was like ingesting joy.

Moving through the garden, I picked two bouquets of broccoli, then gently pulled some baby carrots from the soil, wiped the earth from one and took a bite. Sweet, delicate and crunchy. Everything a carrot should be.

Lightly steamed broccoli with some bright orange carrots and a few onions and radishes to jazz it up – that was going to be supper. We could finish with raspberries and cream for dessert. He would like that. Perhaps I'd put everything on a tray so we could eat outside under the trees.

Seeing the dark, emerald-green zucchinis, I went over to pick a few. Some were slender and elegant, others were thick and turgid, thrusting themselves up and away from the stalk. Maybe tomorrow I'd mix them with some green peppers, tomatoes and fresh basil. Yum.

The scent of wild flowers washed over me, reminding me that I wanted some for the house. In the early spring, I had scattered wild flower seeds and now kaleidoscopes of colour and satisfying fragrances dazzled my senses.

Wild flowers enchanted me. They asked so little, only that I let my eyes appreciate them. The leggy brown-eyed Susans, the virgin-white daisies and lipstick-red poppies, soft, blue cornflowers, all swayed in the warm breezes like groups of girls in summer dance halls. I picked an armful of colour and then, not ready to go up to the house yet, meandered over to my garden chair. Rough and rustic, Harley had made it out of curved willow canes. It looked as if it might belong to a wise old crone in an enchanted forest. I smiled, thinking of him making this "crone chair" for me. Harley seemed to enjoy the idea of me getting old. For him, aging was just another of life's rhythms he was willing to honour.

Now, with the lake lapping just a few yards in front of me and the sweet smells of the flowers wafting up from the basket, I felt contentment breeze through me. Happily, I grazed my bare feet in the moist grasses and listened to the sound of leaves in the wind.

I lifted a postcard from my pocket. On the front was a picture of the Swiss Alps. It was from Norman. After several glorious weeks in Switzerland, he had moved on to other mountains and was planning to "ski my way home, the long way!", the card said. There was no mention of his illness. That didn't mean it wasn't there, but if he were skiing, that was a good sign. He'd decided to live his life full out for a while and see what happened. So far, it looked good.

Norman sounded happy, I thought to myself. Like me. Life had been so satisfying lately. As if I were being rewarded by some invisible benefactor, several opportunities had been offered to me. The first was an invitation to write a book about the tree-saving experience. I was enjoying that immensely. I'd always wanted to write and this was giving me the chance.

What excited me even more was the tree project I had started. A local philanthropist had hired me to be a consultant for a tree-planting venture that involved roaming around the woods for hours, sometimes days. As I often told Charlie who came with me on these jaunts: "If I had a tail, I'd be wagging it."

I looked over the lake. The surface was irresistibly calm. Slipping the postcard into my pocket, I went down to the water for a quick paddle in the canoe. The lake was still. Not brooding but easily still, settled.

Up ahead of my canoe, a loon was calling. I called back to it with what I thought was a rather feeble imitation, but to my surprise, the loon answered and we called back and forth to each other for several minutes. The loon swam closer and looked towards me with great interest. His call became more fervent as our conversation continued.

"I'm a loon trapped in a human's body," I whispered to him.

The loon made a few more celebratory calls, his red eyes examining me piercingly. Then slowly, he swam off, leaving me with the pleasure of being considered one of his kind, if even for a moment.

Quietly, I made my way home, letting the gentle, dripping rhythm of my paddle propel the boat through the water. Back on shore, I deftly turned the canoe over on the grass and sat on the dock, petting Charlie who had waited so patiently on shore.

I heard a laugh from the garden and saw Robyn and her new friend, Patrick, wave as they carried off baskets of raspberries. They were in the process of making jam. I smiled at the thought of Robyn doing such a domestic thing. But Patrick was a down-home type of guy, who had his own gardening business, and the two of them fit together like peas in a pod.

I felt a soft-hearted gratefulness whenever I looked at Robyn these days. Since the incident in the park, she had grown like a repotted plant. She gave her opinion about nearly everything now and her voice was sturdy and substantial. Since she'd met Patrick, she'd been smiling a great deal. Today, over her black tee-shirt, she wore a bright, sun-yellow sweatshirt Patrick had given her.

I sat for a long while on the dock, watching the mesmerizing sparkle of the sunlight on the water. By the time I made my way to the house, I noticed the kids were gone. Back to Patrick's house probably to carry on their project. No doubt a jar or two of jam would appear on my kitchen table in a few days.

I dressed for the concert. It was one of many fund-raising events planned to help the town buy the park. I thought the price Boyd was asking was far too high, but at least we'd forced him to sell. After the confrontation with Robyn, he seemed to have lost interest in his condo project and the subject was never raised again.

There had been lots of gossip about him for a while. Everyone seemed to have a different idea about why he'd backed off the project. Robyn never spoke about it, but I think lots of people figured it out. For a while, there was talk of his wife divorcing him, then talk of them being reconciled. The last I'd heard, Boyd and his wife were thinking of developing a theme park on one of the lakes. I planned to be at the town meeting when that was discussed. I was sure others would be too. With the community watching him, we hoped Boyd wouldn't be able to do much damage.

The Guerrilla Grannies were taking on the fund-raising for the park with their usual zeal, and money was already coming in. Elfy and Agatha were competing to see who could bring in the most. At the moment, Agatha was ahead because Elfy had gone on something called a "vision quest" with Felix. Apparently, Felix is an ex-alcoholic himself and goes on these quests every now and then to keep himself clean. He thought it would do Elfy good and she was game, so they'd gone off a week ago. I was looking forward to seeing her when she got back. The way I figured it, her trip with Felix would give me enough ammunition to pull her leg for at least a year.

Madge became involved in the fund-raising project too. Since she has a lot of time on her hands, she decided to take over some of the work relating to the Earth Elders too. She complains constantly about the old men fawning over her, but I notice she always does her grumbling with a grin. She still goes out with men I don't like very much, but at least she comes home at night to her own house. Sometimes she has a man in tow, but in the morning, she says goodbye and gets on with her day.

I got the sleeping bags ready. After the concert, Harley and I were going to sleep out under the stars. Summer was moving along and we wanted to savour it to the fullest. A meteor shower had started last night and we'd lain naked on our bags watching for hours as bursts of silver shot across the sky like some kind of cosmic orgasm. Tonight was supposed to be even more spectacular.

Our lives were busy, but Harley and I held on to our weekends as sacred offerings to each other. Sometimes he came to my house and sometimes we went away, canoeing deep into the wilds of the north. Harley seemed to know places that only loons and beaver knew, places where the nature spirits were so vibrant I felt the cells in my body dancing as if to music only they could hear.

However much there was to share, Harley and I kept hold of our own lives, each standing firmly on our own ground. Then, like The Lovers in the Park, we reached for heaven together.

Karen Hood-Caddy was born in Toronto, but spent all her summers at the family cottage in Muskoka. After years of travelling and working abroad, she returned to Muskoka, where she does healing work and leads workshops in creativity.

She can be contacted at:
caddy@muskoka.com